THE MANY ADVENTURES OF MEILIN

THE MONKEY KING'S DAUGHTER

BOOK #3

T·A·DeBonis

PUBLISHED BY:
Todd A. DeBonis • DVTVFilm
The Monkey King's Daughter®, is a registered trademark of Todd A. DeBonis (USPTO)

ISBN: 978-0-9678094-5-8   (0-9678094-5-2)

REGISTERED: US Library of Congress, WGA

COVER ILLUSTRATION: John Forcucci, ©2010

WEBSITE: TheMonkeyKingsDaughter.com

ACKNOWLEDGMENTS: Once again, I'm extremely grateful to John Forcucci for his brilliant cover art, Monty Haas and Laurie Joy Haas for their diligent proofing, and all three for their overwhelming encouragement, support and longtime friendship. They are vital to this endeavor and it would not be happening without them. Most importantly, I want to thank my wife, Lien, for still giving me the time to make all this happen— anh yêu em mãi mãi.

PRINTED IN THE USA

For my two girls,
My-Linh and Anna

Chapter 1

The entire Midland Hills High School gymnasium erupted with the roaring thunder of a massive red kettle-shaped Chinese war drum. Accompanying Chinese brass cymbals and iron gongs clashed against the precision beat, creating a haunting metallic, yet festive, eastern rhythm.

Then, amid the crackling bangs and smoke of a string of firecrackers held high on a bamboo pole by a shaggy-haired 22-year-old Asian boy wearing a long-sleeved, black Mandarin-style wushu duangua, two huge Chinese lions, one white and one red, suddenly entered from the double doors at the far end of the gym. They quickly danced and snaked their way to center court to the din of the beat, each lion expertly wielded by members of the touring Monterey He Shan Kung fu Academy.

It took two dancers per lion to manipulate the colorful costumes, one to control the lion's massive head, and the other to control its body and tail. The exhaustive dance also demanded that each performer be in peak physical condition, both acrobatically and with their Kung fu. The Lion Dance was as much a display of beauty and grace as it was of disciplined martial arts ability.

It was Friday—two days before Chinese New Year—the Year of the Tiger, and the beginning of the February school break. The program was being sponsored by the California high school to both celebrate the holiday honoring the town's Asian population, as well as a colorful, fun and educational school event designed to broaden cultural awareness.

"This is awesome!" Jessie Macintyre squealed above the thunder of the drum, as the lions bobbed their massive heads, blinked their enormous glittering eyes, and danced their way about the gymnasium floor.

"What's this called again?" the bubbly brown-haired fourteen-year-old freshman asked her best friend.

"Wu Shi!" an equally thrilled Meilin Cheng replied. Lion Dancing was one of her favorite Chinese New Year's events.

"Wu shee? Jessie repeated.

"Means Lion Dance," Meilin added.

"Duh!" Jessie remarked, making her *duh* face. "I kind'a figured that. How old is it?"

"Real old. Like, thousands."

"What's with the fruit and vegetables?" Jessie asked, referring to the two plates of food placed on the gym floor near the center row of the telescoping wall bleachers the two girls sat on. The blond-colored wooden bleachers ran the full length of both sides of the gym and were packed full with the entire student body.

"That's the lions' reward," Meilin explained. "Hidden inside the heads of lettuce is some money. It's kind of like an offering to the lions for giving their blessings and dispelling evil. They must eat the food in order to get their reward. If this was a competition between two wushi schools, the lion dancers who performed best would be awarded a prize."

"This kind'a stuff go on back in—*you-know-where?*" Jessie asked, finishing the *you-know-where* with a hushed voice, referring to Meilin's ancient past and the legendary land of the Heavenly Kingdom, the Jade Emperor, and Meilin's father, Sun Wukong, the Monkey King.

"Yup," Meilin smiled. "But back there, the demon lions are real!"

3

"Real?" Jessie gulped.

Meilin's face widened with a broad smile. "Yeah, so ya don't wanna be stingy with the cash—or the food."

"And if you are?"

"Bad luck," Meilin said. She then added with a grin, "And they eat you!"

Jessie swallowed hard. "I'm so glad we live in the 21st century."

Meilin chuckled. "Yeah, me too!" she said. Meilin *did* like living her life in the 21st century with all the modern comforts and electronic entertainment that went along with it. But the pretty 14-year-old Asian-American teen was also experiencing life in the past as well, and learning to like the simpler, though somewhat more disciplined, life of her ancestors. There was something to be said for both time periods and she was grateful that she could freely travel between them—though her previous sojourns back in Time to the era of the Monkey King were less than idyllic, to say the least. There was a hefty price on Meilin's head, dead or alive—and no lack of demon bounty hunters who wanted to collect. Demon Bull King and his minions, although thwarted by her father and the Jade Emperor's celestial warriors, were not totally defeated. They vowed revenge and it didn't matter which time period it occurred in—then or now.

The two friends turned their attention back to the dancers on the floor just in time to see one of the oranges the red lion scooped up in its large mouth come flying at them.

"Look out!" Meilin cried, intercepting the orange in her left hand just before it would have struck Jessie in her face.

"Hey!" Jessie griped. "You didn't say they spit their food at the spectators!"

Meilin laughed. "You're supposed to catch it! If a lion tosses you one of the oranges, it means you'll have good luck this year."

"Cool!" Jessie beamed, taking the orange from her friend's hand. "I can use some of that! It would be cool to find a twenty in my baloney sandwich at lunchtime, too!" she added, watching both lions greedily gobble the heads of lettuce from their offering plates and spew the shredded leaves from their massive jaws across the gym floor.

"Those guys can really chow down," Meilin remarked.

"Kind'a like your Uncle Zhu at an all-you-can eat buffet." Jessie quipped, referring to Meilin's guardian uncle, who was actually the legendary

Zhu Bajie—Pigsy the Pig. "OMG! That didn't come out right," she quickly said apologetically.

Meilin laughed. "It's true. There isn't a demon lion born that can out-eat my uncle—or make a bigger mess doing it! Last night, after he closed his shop," Meilin continued, referring to her uncle's downtown *Heavenly River Imports* shop, an odd collection of Asian antiques, curiosities and tacky Asian kitsch, "we drove over to the Golden Dragon Buffet on Main Street. As soon as we got out of the car, you could see the owners and staff frantically scurrying about through the glass windows, removing the expensive dishes from the steam tables. One of them even tried to put a CLOSED sign on the door just as we reached it. It was *so* funny!"

Jessie giggled at the thought. "Yeah, your uncle can wipe out a $9.95 buffet in about an hour."

"And he did," Meilin added. "Totally wiped them out."

"Seriously?" Jessie said, with raised eyebrows. "I thought he was on a diet."

"Seriously!" Meilin confirmed. "And *that is* his diet!"

Both girls laughed as the drums suddenly got louder. They returned their attention to the lions, as the troop concluded their dance with a flurry of Kung fu stances and footwork.

Everyone in the gym applauded wildly. Everyone, that is, except Meilin's nemesis—stuck-up, blue-eyed, blond-beauty, Tiffany Edwards, and two of her inner circle of Tiffany wannabes, Samantha and Mackenzie. Tiffany's face remained steadfastly cold. Samantha almost applauded, and Meilin could see that she wanted to, but stopped and lowered her hands when Tiffany gave her an icy glare.

Tiffany had a great knack for manipulating people and social events. If she wasn't the center of attention—no one was. And that was fine with Meilin. She didn't want to draw any attention to herself anyway, especially in light of her newfound identity.

Later, while filing back through the hallways after the program concluded to collect their belongings from their lockers for the bus trip home, Tiffany grumbled just loud enough for Meilin to hear, "Chinese New Year—what a bogus holiday! Everybody knows New Year's Day is January 1st."

She then turned her gaze toward Meilin and scoffed, "But then again, what do you expect from people who eat their food with wooden sticks."

Meilin forced a thin smile. Five months ago, any one of the many disparaging remarks Tiffany routinely insulted her with would have hurt her, possibly even made her cry. But not anymore. Meilin knew quite well who she was, knew about her incredible ancient heritage, and she was darn proud of it. There was nothing Tiffany could ever do or say that could hurt her anymore. But that didn't mean she didn't want to enjoy everything that high school life had to offer, and that included having friends—maybe even one day, a boyfriend.

Jessie, however, wasn't so forgiving. Bullies like Tiffany easily ticked her off. She was the only one outside Meilin's family who knew who Meilin really was—and what her friend was capable of doing. Meilin was the Monkey King's daughter. She could squash Tiffany like a bug with her superhuman abilities, and Jessie, though sometimes envious of those abilities, was glad the burden and responsibilities of being the Monkey King's daughter didn't rest on her shoulders. Having to fight demons at every turn had its disadvantages—mainly, the very real possibility of being killed. Still, the flying was cool—that, and Meilin being able to turn into anything or anyone she wanted. Jessie definitely could put that ability to good use, especially on April Fool's Day.

"What's that supposed to mean!" Jessie growled.

Tiffany looked around, as if searching for the source of the remark. "Did you girls hear something?"

"Some kind'a puking sound?" the Tiffany-clone named Mackenzie scoffed.

"No," Tiffany replied. "More like the barking sound a circus seal makes when it wants a fish. No wait," she said as her gaze settled on Jessie and Meilin. "Oh, my mistake. It's only *chopstick* and her little dweeb. We're so proud of you," Tiffany directed condescendingly at Meilin. "Taking the time to teach the dweeb to speak. It must be such a good feeling, helping the helpless."

Jessie grit her teeth and took a half-step forward, but Meilin stayed her, placing her hand firmly on her friend's shoulder.

"Did you ever find out how all those rats got in your locker?" Meilin smiled, referring to the hundred large rats that came pouring out of Tiffany's locker only several weeks ago. Meilin magically created the rats from a few tufts of her demon monkey fur—payback for the time Tiffany and her posse deliberately sabotaged her chances to befriend a recent good-looking transfer student who showed interest in her.

Tiffany's eyes narrowed. She hadn't forgotten the humiliating event that, according to school officials and the expensive exterminators they were forced to hire, never happened. No traces or evidence of rats or any other kind of vermin were ever found—for which the staff in the cafeteria were extremely grateful, as well as the teachers and students who ate there. School officials concluded that Tiffany and her posse made the whole thing up to garner attention, though they couldn't prove it.

"I mean," Meilin continued, as she spun the dial on her own combination lock and opened her locker door, "you never know what you might find in these lockers. Snakes. Roaches. A skunk... The school's old, right? Could be all kinds of things crawling around inside these walls."

Meilin shrugged innocently at Tiffany as she deposited her books on the shelf, grabbed her jacket and swung her locker door shut.

Meilin then winked at Jessie, who fell in step with her friend and the two headed down the hall toward the exit and the waiting busses.

As they passed Tiffany's locker, Meilin covertly wiggled the index finger of her right hand, magically causing Tiffany's locker door to rattle, as if something big and nasty were inside. The sudden noise made Tiffany and her two wannabes jump with trepidation.

Jessie struggled to contain herself from laughing.

"Oh," Meilin said, pausing mid-stride, "and as far as your crack about eating with chopsticks goes... It's a skill we developed 5000 years ago. In fact, it wasn't 'til about 400 years ago that your European ancestors stopped eating their food with their hands—which, I'm guessing, was just about the time *your* particular lineage probably learned to walk upright."

"Ooo, nice burn!" Jessie giggled as the two girls smartly turned their backs on Tiffany and her posse and walked away. Meilin magically gave Tiffany's locker door one more rattle for good measure that made the three girls jump again. There was no way that Tiffany would open her locker door now.

"If I ever find out that it was you!" Tiffany called after Meilin defiantly.

Meilin acknowledged Tiffany's pointless threat by holding her left arm up in the air and making the "L" loser sign with her fingers.

"Wow, look at the *new* Meilin. You *go* girl!" Jessie remarked with delight.

"I'm just tired of her dopey insults, that's all!" Meilin replied, with a hint of exhaustion in her voice. She never wanted to use her magic on anyone without just cause, especially in *this* world, where the notion of magic was decidedly extraordinary. First, it was against her Tao. Secondly, it was dangerous. *"Magic,"* her uncle Zhu warned repeatedly, *"is like a GPS signal that pinpoints your location, making it easy for Demon Bull King or his minions to find you."*

"You two are gonna have a showdown someday," Jessie said prophetically.

"No we're not," Meilin countered with conviction, denying the inevitable. "I'm not a threat to her, or her plans to become homecoming queen, prom queen—or whatever sort'a *queen* she wants to be. I'm as low on the social totem pole as it gets."

"Yeah, well, for some reason, I'm guessing she thinks you *are*," Jessie countered. "Why else would she have it in for you?"

"I honestly don't know," Meilin acknowledged. And she didn't. But it was Chinese New Year and Meilin was resolved not to let thoughts of Tiffany Edwards spoil any of that.

"So," Meilin said, changing the tone of the conversation to a happier one as she and Jessie climbed the steps of their bus. "You wanna come over later tonight? My mom's gonna cook up some bao—you know, those steamed buns you like with the meat and egg in them?"

"You bet!" Jessie said emphatically. She loved those buns—that was a fact. But would she actually get any with Meilin's uncle Zhu sitting at the same table? He could pop the meaty dumplings down his throat like they were *M&Ms.*

"And we can listen to the new *Justin Bieber* CD I got!" Jessie added excitedly.

"*Juh-stin!*" both girls squealed in unison as they took their seats midway back in the bus, Jessie sitting at the window.

"I *love* him!" Meilin stated emphatically as the bus started rolling.

"Me, too! He's *so* hot!" Jessie agreed, then her face dropped. "Ah, poop!" she grumbled.

"What?" Meilin asked, noting her friend's sudden sour expression.

"My grandma's coming to visit."

"The one you don't like?" Meilin asked.

"No, the one who doesn't like *me!*" Jessie countered.

"Same thing," Meilin restated.

"Yeah..." Jessie reluctantly agreed. "I really can't stand her," she then added. "She's always riding my mom—never has anything good to say about my dad. Doesn't care about me or my brother. Heck, I don't even know why she bothers visiting. I try to be good, ya know—make her happy," Jessie continued. "But nothing I do seems to matter. It's like she hates us or something." Jessie shifted her gaze to the passing scenery. "That's why I hate her, too."

Meilin looked at her friend and frowned. Having ill feelings about family was tough—something Meilin knew firsthand. She grew up with the frustration of not knowing anything about her father, her grandmother—anyone. It was just Meilin, her mom and her uncle Zhu. Luckily, they gave her all the love they could. But still, sometimes even that wasn't enough. At least Jessie had relatives. Meilin just found out who her father, her grandmother and the rest of her relatives were only a few months ago, and that was a shock in itself. But to grow up in a family knowing that your own grandmother didn't like you...

"You know," Meilin said. "Maybe things will be different this time. I mean, she *does* visit. That must mean something..."

Jessie simply shrugged.

Meilin wrinkled her nose with frustration—then she smiled. She reached into her backpack and fished out a small rectangular red packet and handed it to Jessie.

"Here, this is for you," Meilin said.

"What is it?" Jessie asked, taking the red packet in her hands, studying it. The front was emblazoned with an ornate picture of a golden tiger and Chinese logograms that said Happy New Year.

"It's a Hóng Bāo," Meilin explained. "A Chinese tradition. We give them to family and friends on New Year's—for good luck. Go ahead, open it!"

Jessie smiled and opened the little envelope. Her eyes widened. There was a neatly folded, crisp twenty-dollar bill inside.

"Jeez, Meilin," Jessie gasped, not knowing what to say.

"It's not a baloney sandwich, but—Happy New Year," Meilin beamed.

"Well, yeah," Jessie sputtered. "Happy New Year. But I can't take this..." she said, handing the red packet back.

"You got to," Meilin insisted. "Bad luck if you don't. Besides, you're family now," Meilin added. Indeed, Meilin considered Jessie much more than her BFF. Jessie was like a sister—especially since she knew Meilin's secret. And, since Meilin considered her so, it was time to include her in her cultural family traditions.

Jessie's face widened with a smile. "Okay. Don't wanna argue with tradition. Besides, a girl needs all the luck she can get, right?"

"That's for sure," Meilin affirmed with a nod. She then paused and shifted her gaze out the window. Their bus was nearing its stop at the street corner where she and Jessie lived. Jessie's house was two driveways down from the corner. There was an ambulance parked in her driveway with its red lights flashing. Meilin could see her own mother, Lijuan, and her Uncle Zhu Bajie standing near the rear of the ambulance as two EMT's came out of Jessie's house bearing a stretcher.

Jessie picked up on Meilin's expression.

"What?" she asked, turning her head in the direction Meilin was staring.

"Oh my God!" Jessie gasped. She bolted over Meilin and scrambled for the front exit of the school bus as the driver barely pulled to a stop. Meilin was close on her heels.

"Mom!" Jessie wailed as she ran toward her house, her heart pounding, fearing the worst.

When Jessie reached the ambulance, her mother emerged from her home. The ambulance wasn't there for her. *"Thank God!"* Jessie's mind screamed. But, if the ambulance wasn't there for her mom, then who was it there for?

"Grandma!" Jessie blurted out.

Jessie ran to her mother, who embraced her.

"Grandma's suffered a stroke," Jessie's mother Grace said, with a shaky voice. "I'm going to the hospital. I want you to stay here!"

"No!" Jessie replied defiantly. "I'm going with you!"

"I need you to stay!" Grace insisted. "Your dad's picking up your brother at day school. I want you here when they get home."

"No!" Jessie cried. "I'm going!" She then turned and faced Meilin's mother. "Mrs. Cheng, you can watch Kevin when he gets home, can't you?" she pleaded with tears in her eyes.

"Of course," Lijuan replied. She then looked at Grace and nodded.

"Okay, fine!" Jessie's mother relented. To Lijuan she mouthed, "Thank you..."

And that was it. Jessie and her mother hopped into the rear of the ambulance. An EMT closed the door and within seconds, the ambulance raced away, its siren blaring.

Meilin stood by her mother, clutching her hand as the ambulance disappeared from sight.

"You can heal her, right?" Meilin said turning her face up toward her mom.

Lijuan took a moment before gazing down at her daughter.

"No," Lijuan said. There was deep regret in her voice.

"But Mom!" Meilin countered. "You're a healer! I've seen you bring back people who were virtually dead!"

Lijuan exhaled softly and closed her eyes for a long moment. "I'm sorry," she said, opening her eyes again. "But, I can't."

Lijuan then turned and walked slowly toward the Cheng home.

"Can't?" Meilin cried with confusion. "Or won't!"

Lijuan didn't answer.

Meilin turned to face her uncle Zhu. The tremendously large man draped an arm around Meilin and turned her toward their home.

"She can fix this!" Meilin stated with conviction as they began to walk. "I *know* she can fix this!"

"Yes, she can," Zhu Bajie said softly. "But she won't."

"Why?" Meilin demanded.

"Because it's against the Tao."

Chapter 2

"Against the Tao?" Meilin sputtered, confronting her mother in their living room. Lijuan was standing in front of the family's small wooden butsudan, holding three smoldering yellow joss sticks to her forehead. She didn't answer her daughter. Instead she continued whispering her Buddhist prayer, while bowing three times. This only added to Meilin's frustration.

"Mom!" Meilin continued. "Jessie's my best friend! You gotta do something!"

"I *am* doing something," Lijuan said calmly, after she was finished. She placed her joss sticks in the tiny sand-filled bowl located on the altar in front of the small statuette of Buddha so they would remain upright and not fall over. She then bowed slightly to another statuette sitting to the left of Buddha—a statuette of her husband,

Meilin's father, Sun Wukong—the Monkey King. She then turned and faced Meilin. "I'm praying for her soul."

Meilin stared at her mother, her mouth agape. She couldn't believe what she was hearing.

"Now," Lijuan said, her voice still calm and collected. "I've got bao to make."

"*Bao?*" Meilin repeated. "How can you make bao when Jessie's grandma's dying!"

"I know, Meilin. Believe me, I know." The strikingly beautiful Asian woman then nodded to Zhu Bajie to 'take over' as she walked from the room.

Meilin turned to her uncle, waiting for any insight that would explain her mother's incredulous indifference.

Zhu Bajie carried his massive frame over to the pale green living room couch and sat down. He motioned for Meilin to join him at the other end.

Meilin didn't move. Instead, she crossed her arms across her chest and waited for her uncle to speak.

Zhu Bajie took a long, thoughtful breath. "Your mother can't help Jessie's grandmother because it's her '*time*'..."

Meilin opened her mouth to object to her uncle's opening statement. Zhu Bajie raised a hand, indicating that she at least wait until he was finished before chiming in.

"My old friend Lao Tzu once said, *'Life and death are one thread, the same line viewed from different sides,'*" Zhu Bajie recited.

Meilin rolled her eyes—another one of Lao's enigmatic wisdoms her uncle was always quoting that she was somehow supposed to interpret. Zhu sensed her impatience and cut to the quick.

"Think of yourself as a flower. You come into this world born of a seed. You grow tall, reaching for the sun, full of Yang. You reach maturity, flower, and hopefully produce your own seed to carry on in your place. Your Yang is replaced by your Yin, you grow old, whither and die. It's the perpetual cycle of the Tao—the true nature of The Way. Your mother will never violate it."

"But, Uncle Z," Meilin countered, "Mom does it all the time. When Hóng Hái-Er attacked Shuilian-dong," Meilin continued, referring to the Red Boy's recent attack on her Demon Monkey homeland, "She was right there, healing the injured children and soldiers, saving lives."

"Yes, she was," Zhu Bajie agreed. "And so were you," he reminded.

"Well then?" Meilin stated.

"Not the same thing," Zhu Bajie replied. "Even though those children and soldiers were severely injured, they were still full of life. Their Yang dominated their *Ch'i*—their internal life essence, and your mother used that to heal them. Jessie's grandmother's Yang has dissipated. Her Yin has replaced it by its own true nature. This isn't something your mother will reverse. It would be against Nature."

"So, what you're saying is—when your natural time's up—it's up? That's it? Nadda? Caput? It's over?"

"Pretty much," Zhu Bajie nodded.

"Hmph! That's easy for you to say, you're immortal," Meilin growled.

Zhu Bajie frowned. "Don't confuse immortality with the nature of the Tao. Enlightenment and immortality are but phases one can attain on the journey we're *all* taking—demon or human."

Zhu Bajie could see that his words were not resonating with Meilin.

"Nature isn't human-hearted, Meilin," Zhu Bajie said bluntly. "Nor is death something to be feared. Death is as much a part of life as life is of death. They're absolute compliments of each other. It's the natural order of things. Yin flows into Yang and Yang flows into Yin. To interfere is to corrupt."

"But it's Jessie's grandmother!" Meilin restated, as if that mere fact would override her uncle's words.

"I know," Zhu Bajie said. "And it's hard. But the best thing you can do is *be there* for your friend—help her through her grief."

"No," Meilin countered, her eyes watering slightly. "This isn't right. We should do something—*everything* we *can* to keep her alive— no matter what!"

Zhu Bajie sighed heavily and was about to go on when the front doorbell interrupted.

"We'll talk more about this later," Zhu Bajie said, lifting his massive body up from the couch. "It's really important you fully grasp what I'm saying," he said as he walked from the living room to the hallway and opened the front door.

It was Jessie's father, Eric, and little Kevin.

"Hey, Kevin," Zhu Bajie said with a broad smile while reaching over the small brown-haired 4-year-old to shake Eric Macintyre's hand. "How's my favorite little skate-boarder?"

"Dad says I gotta stay here 'cause my Grammy's sick," Kevin stated flatly.

"That's cool with you, right?" Zhu Bajie replied.

"Guess so..." Kevin grunted.

"We have popcorn," Zhu Bajie offered. Kevin's face instantly lit up. Then he paused and looked up at the big man.

"How much popcorn?" he asked point-blank. For a little guy, he well knew Zhu Bajie's eating style.

"Whole new jar," Zhu Bajie reassured. "It's in the kitchen. Why don't you go get it. Mrs. Cheng will find you a pot and the oil. And I'll be right there to get it started."

Kevin didn't need to be told twice. He pushed his way past Zhu Bajie as Meilin appeared at the door. She forced a smile.

"How, um, is, ah..." Meilin asked awkwardly.

"We don't know," Jessie's father returned. "I talked to Grace on my cell phone," he said, looking away slightly. "Doesn't look good..."

"I'm sorry," Zhu Bajie said sincerely. "If there's anything we can do..."

"Watching Kevin's a big help," he said. Then he added, "I should get going."

"Of course," Zhu Bajie nodded. "We're here if you need us."

Eric Macintyre returned the nod, then turned and walked quickly toward his car, its engine still idling in the Cheng's driveway.

Zhu Bajie closed the front door, only to find Meilin staring up at him. There was anger in her voice.

"By *'anything'* —you mean *'nothing'!*" she remarked accusingly.

"Meilin," Zhu Bajie said with a weary sigh. He was interrupted.

"Hey, Big Z!" Kevin called from the far end of the hall. Big Z was his nickname for the over 300-pound man. "You comin'? This stuff don't pop itself!"

Chapter 3

"How long does she have?" Meilin asked. It was 9PM. She was sitting on the edge of Jessie's bed in the upstairs bedroom of her friend's house. Jessie sat in a slump next to her. Her eyes were swollen and red from crying.

"Before she dies? They don't know. A couple of days if we're lucky," Jessie sniffled. "What kind'a *luck* is that!" Her tears began to flow down her cheeks again.

Meilin put her arms around her friend and hugged her close. It was all she could do to keep from crying herself.

"I said I hated her," Jessie sobbed. "And I don't! I love her. Maybe if I was nicer, none of this would've happened. And now I can't tell her I'm sorry... Oh, Meilin... What can I do?"

"I don't know," Meilin said softly. "But there's gotta be something."

"What about your mom?" Jessie suddenly thought. "Isn't there some kind of Chinese medicine in her shop she can give her?"

Meilin shook her head, no. In truth, there might be an herb, or combination of herbs among the literally hundreds of dried medicinal plants, mushrooms and other mysterious items that Lijuan stored in her apothecary below Zhu Bajie's *Heavenly River Imports* shop, that might help. But even if there were, Meilin didn't know where to begin to look. And even if she did find a tincture or concoction of some kind, what could she do with it? Despite growing up surrounded by her mother's healing art, she never paid any real attention to it. Besides, Lijuan already made it perfectly clear that she wouldn't intervene. There was nothing she could do. Or, *would* do...

"There's gotta be something!" Meilin thought again, racking her brain for a solution. She was the Monkey King's daughter. She could do everything her father could do. Her developing powers and ability were beyond anything that she could imagine. But for all her father's magic and fighting skill, he wasn't a healer. And that meant that Meilin wasn't one either.

Or was she?

"I'm only half demon monkey," Meilin reasoned. *"I'm also half fae. Mom's healing ability might be in me as well. But how do I evoke it?"*

How, indeed! Meilin's fighting skills were intuitive, with new abilities thus far manifesting only when the need arose—such as her immanent death, or through rigorous practice with a teacher like cranky old Zhang, the Taoist Master her father retained to train her.

"Of course!" Meilin said out loud.

"What?" Jessie said mid-sniffle.

"What a doof!" she said standing, admonishing herself for not seeing the obvious sooner.

Jessie stared blankly up at Meilin, not knowing what to make of her sudden flash of exuberance.

"Look," Meilin explained. "My mom says there isn't anything *she* can do, but that doesn't mean something can't be done! It's so clear!" Meilin exclaimed, almost jumping for joy.

"What?" Jessie asked, caught up in Meilin's energy.

"My mom had to learn her healing art from someone, right? All I gotta do is go through the Gate, find out who it was—and get them to teach me!"

"And if they won't?"

"Hey," Meilin boasted confidently. "I'm Princess Meilin of the Demon Monkey Kingdom—daughter of Sun Wukong, the Monkey King. You seriously think they'd say no?"

"But Meilin..." Jessie started.

"It's probably someone from my mom's home village—a shaman or some Taoist master," Meilin rambled on, not listening to her friend.

"Meilin!" Jessie repeated again, this time more forcefully as she took hold of Meilin's shoulders and lightly shook her.

"What?" Meilin said with surprise.

"The Gate!" Jessie said, referring to the ancient wooden Chinese Gate located in the rear of Zhu Bajie's shop that was actually a magical portal to Meilin's mystical past. It was the very gate created by Sun Wukong and Meilin's grandmother, Guan Yin, to save his newborn daughter and his wife from the clutches of Demon Bull King, sending them forward in time, well over 3000 years ago.

"You can't use the Gate without your mom's or your Uncle Z's permission, remember?"

Jessie was right. Using the Gate without permission was forbidden—especially after Meilin's previous near-fatal encounter with Red Boy.

"Hmph!" Meilin grunted. Her exuberance deflated. She returned to Jessie's bed and sat heavily on the corner of the mattress.

Jessie sat down next to her.

"Well, it was almost a good idea."

"Yeah..." Meilin muttered. Jessie was right. Neither her mother nor her uncle would give her permission to use the Gate for this, especially after they'd told her there was nothing they could do.

The two girls sat in silence. Tears began to trickle from Jessie's eyes again and run down her cheeks.

"Sorry," she said, wiping her face, embarrassed by her lack of control.

Meilin nodded understandingly. For all of Jessie's outward toughness, she was really a softy inside.

Meilin turned her head away and stared down at the floor. Watching her best friend bear this much pain was too much to take—she just had to do *something*.

Meilin absentmindedly began to finger the small jade Monkey King pendant that hung from the delicate black Chinese silk cord that she wore around her neck. The necklace was a gift from her Uncle Zhu. *"A little somethin' to remind you who you are,"* he said when he gave it to her. *"In case you ever have doubts..."*

"I know who I am," Meilin thought. *"For all the good it does anyone..."*

Meilin abruptly shot to her feet again.

"Nope! This is wrong—all wrong," she muttered as she walked swiftly to Jessie's bedroom window. She easily threw the lower window up with the flick of a finger. "Stay strong. I'll be back!" she said, looking back at Jessie. Meilin then morphed herself into a small sparrow and in a flash of feathers, flew out the window.

Just as she flew away, there was a light knock on Jessie's bedroom door.

"Meilin," Zhu Bajie called softly as he pushed the door open. He and Lijuan had been downstairs visiting Jessie's parents, offering their support while Meilin was upstairs with her friend.

"It's time to go home—let everyone here get some sleep."

Zhu Bajie's face dropped.

No Meilin.

Zhu Bajie looked at Jessie—then at the open window—then back at Jessie. The look on Jessie's face told him everything he needed to know.

"Dang it, Meilin!" he grumbled disapprovingly.

Chapter 4

When Zhu Bajie and Lijuan burst through the front door of Zhu's antique shop, Meilin was already standing under the wooden frame of the open Gate in the back of the store. In her hands were the three magical keys her grandmother, Guan Yin, had bequeathed to her as a baby—her three jade hair sticks. They were the only keys that could unlock the ancient Gate's magical portal between the two worlds.

"Meilin! You stop right there!" Lijuan ordered.

"We know what you're thinking—and you're wrong! " Zhu Bajie added.

"No!" Meilin cried. "What's *wrong*—is *not* to try!"

"Meilin!" Lijuan desperately implored. "Listen to me! If something could humanly be done, we'd do it. But it can't. Now I'm telling you for the last time, do NOT step through that Gate!"

"Sorry, Mom!" Meilin replied, stepping halfway into the swirling vortex that would send her back in Time. "But I gotta. You'll see. I'm right about this!"

"Zhu!" Lijuan commanded with frustration, motioning that he physically stop Meilin.

Zhu Bajie instantly morphed himself into his true form—that of the legendary Pigsy the Pig, so he could cross the room faster than his clumsy mortal human guise could.

But he wasn't quick enough.

Meilin fully stepped into the dark, swirling magical vortex, and vanished.

The Gate's two wooden doors slammed shut of their own accord, its rusty lock snapping securely into place, just as Zhu Bajie reached it.

"Argh!" Zhu Bajie spat with frustration. His nine-toothed rake of pure ice metal instantly materialized in his hands and he brought the weapon crashing down on the lock with a tremendous "*He-ya!*"

It was a futile gesture. The demon pig knew nothing magical or otherwise could break the lock.

Meilin was gone, and there was nothing he or Lijuan could do about it.

All they could hope for was that Meilin would come to her senses and return before she did anything foolish—or worse.

- - - - - - - - - - - - - - -

When Meilin stepped through the Gate on the other side, she was met with the bewildered face of Shirong, a stoop-shouldered elder demon monkey whom her father appointed Regent to oversee the demon Monkey Kingdom during his or Lijuan's absence. Shirong was exceptionally ancient in years and had known Meilin's father when they both were very young. He was, in fact, one of the demon monkeys who dared a young Sun WuKong to plunge through the waterfall that concealed Water Curtain Cave and return alive— thus securing his rightful place as the Monkey King. That was over 3,000 years ago by Meilin's timeline.

"Princess," Shirong said, bowing his head. "New Year's festivities don't begin 'til the day after tomorrow. We didn't expect to see you before then..." The old demon monkey paused, eyeing the Gate. The wooden doors were shut and locked. "And without your mother or Zhu Bajie," he continued, taking note of their conspicuous absence. Shirong well knew that Meilin was to be escorted everywhere she went.

"Um, well, holiday time, you know," Meilin quickly fabricated as she casually poked her three jade hair sticks into her ponytail knot. "Last minute things to take care of. So they sent me on ahead..."

Shirong studied Meilin for a long moment. He then bowed his wizened grey-whiskered head once more. He could easily tell by Meilin's body language that something was amiss. But he would not challenge her word.

"As you say, Princess," he smiled. "Well, now that you're here, why not accompany me to the nursery. The young ones are just going to sleep. They'll be ever so glad to see you. They've been working very hard to prepare songs for the New Year's celebration. Very hard, indeed. They'd love to know you've arrived early."

"Sounds wonderful," Meilin replied with warm honesty. She adored the demon monkey children as much as they adored her. Their company had become the highlight of her visits.

"But, let's let them sleep. It's late and they need their rest."

Shirong nodded once more and held up his arm, gesturing toward the path that led toward the center chamber of the massive cave that was their home.

"We're hoping that your father will be able to join us this year," Shirong went on. "That is, of course, if he's not busy with matters concerning the Court," he said, referring to the Heavenly Court of the Jade Emperor.

Meilin nodded. It *would* be good if she could see her father. He'd know exactly what to do or who to see regarding Jessie's grandmother. But the likelihood of that happening was remote. Sun Wukong was rarely available to her, especially with the rumors that the exiled Demon Bull King was secretly attempting to amass his forces once more.

Shirong and Meilin continued their way into the massive main chamber of Shuilian-dong.

"Sifu," Meilin said, using the venerable term for *teacher* as they walked past the many demon monkeys who inhabited the cave. Each bowed a silent greeting of respect for Meilin as she passed.

"Yes, Princess?" the old monkey replied.

"My mother's a great healer, isn't she?" Meilin said.

"Indeed! Very much like her own mother in that respect."

Meilin smiled. Lijuan was the daughter of Guan Yin, Goddess of Mercy. And though Meilin only met her grandmother once—during the time of her first journey to her past when she discovered who she really was—it was a magical moment that she'll never forget. Would Meilin ever see her again? She hoped so. Had Guan Yin not appeared to Meilin in her moment of despair, she might not have found the courage to go on.

"It must've taken her years to learn."

"Indeed."

Meilin nodded, then reflected, "And she must've had a wonderful teacher."

"Indeed, she did. Several, in fact."

"Hmm. I wonder if *I* could ever become a healer like my mom," Meilin pondered.

"Indeed, I'm sure you could, Princess," Shirong said again.

Meilin smiled. Shirong had a habit of saying *indeed* a lot.

"You are, after all, half fae," he continued.

"But not all fae are healers."

"This is true," Shirong agreed. He then paused. "Is there some reason your Highness asks me this? Are you ill? If so, I'll summon a shaman at once..."

"No-no, nothing like that," Meilin reassured the elder. "I just thought that it would be cool if I could learn some of the art myself—you know, in case something ever came up."

"The path of a healer is a worthy one, indeed," Shirong *indeeded* again.

"But a very long path..."

"Indeed—especially if one wishes to become a master."

"Indeed," Meilin *indeeded* herself now. This *indeeding* was contagious. "And of all the healing techniques, which do you think would be the most difficult to learn?"

"Well, that would be the Healing Hand."

"Healing Hand?"

"Indeed. Very few can master it."

"Indeed," Meilin replied, trying to keep a straight face. "But not impossible."

"Indeed."

The two continued their walk.

"Whoever taught my mother the technique must surely be great."

"Indeed," Shirong said. "She was instructed by the Abbess of Cloud Valley Monastery herself."

"Oh yeah, that's right! The monastery in the hills, just south of Dragon Mountain."

"No," Shirong replied. "Cloud Valley is northeast of here, over the Mountain of Five Elements, toward the fae island of Penglai."

"Of course," Meilin said, clapping her hands lightly together for effect. "I remember my mom telling me that now," she lied. Meilin then shrugged, "Dragon Mountain, Fire Mountain, Five Elements Mountain—still haven't got all that straight in my head yet."

Meilin paused near a mound of glittering stalagmite and took a seat on the rock. She took a deep breath and placed her hand to her head. "Sifu, would it be possible for me to have something to drink? The trip through the Gate seems to have made me a bit light-headed..."

"Oh, heavens! My apologies! How could I be so neglectful," Shirong admonished himself. "I'll fetch you something this instant! Mango juice. No—pear... Yes, pear. That would be best."

Shirong scurried off as fast as his old legs could carry him. "Neglectful," he muttered as he went. "Neglectful, indeed..."

"Thank you, Sifu," Meilin called after him. She then whispered to herself, "Thank you, *indeed*."

As soon as Shirong disappeared from view, Meilin was up and on the move. She made her way quickly toward the mouth of the cave.

Meilin then hurried across the narrow covered monkey bridge that the demon monkeys constructed so they could pass through the 1500-foot waterfall that tumbled down Mount Huagou without getting wet. She smiled at the guards at each end of the bridge.

"Beautiful night," Meilin commented as she passed their posts.

"Princess," each would say in agreement, with a clasped-hand-over-fist salute.

Outside, Meilin skirted the rocky edge of the large pool at the base of the mountain until she reached a small clearing nearby.

Meilin then conjured a small flying cloud, stepped on it and flew straight up into the night sky, heading northeast for Five Elements Mountain.

Or, so she thought...

Chapter 5

It didn't take long before Meilin began to wonder if she was flying in the right direction. *"Northeast"* was the heading Shirong mentioned, and if Meilin were any judge of speed and direction—which she wasn't—or if she could navigate by the stars above—which she couldn't—Five Elements Mountain should have come into view by now.

But it didn't.

Instead, the terrain below her was moderately flat, alternately covered with thick bamboo forest and a mixture of scrub grass and pine. The land below was also unpopulated—not so much as even a farm.

"Poop!" she cussed under her breath.

"Should I go back?" Meilin wondered. If she did, a very upset Shirong would be waiting for her. The old demon monkey would demand that she

open the Gate which would allow either Zhu Bajie, her mother, or both to come through—and that was *definitely not* what she needed to deal with at all. Plus, going back now wouldn't help Jessie *or* her grandmother. No, she had to press on, find a village or farm, land and ask directions.

"Where's triple-A when you need them," Meilin quipped aloud to herself. *"One of their maps would be nice—or even a printout of a* Google *satellite view."* But all of those handy conveniences were at least 3000 years in the future.

"Might as well be three million years," she knew.

And then Meilin saw it. In the distance, the dark shape of a large mountain loomed against what was now a predawn sky. At the base of the mountain, there was a cluster of lights—hanging lanterns actually, swaying gently back and forth in the night wind.

"Finally," Meilin thought, breathing a sigh of relief. She made a quick motion with her hand, directing her flying cloud to descend and head toward the lights and what appeared to be a small village.

Meilin landed her flying cloud in the center of the village square. The cloud vanished into a wisp of fog around her feet as she dismissed it.

Meilin's demon monkey-senses tingled. Something was amiss here. The town was quiet— too quiet.

Even for a remote village, there were always guards or, at the very least, a night watchman walking the streets. This place looked like a ghost town in an old western movie, minus the obligatory tumbleweed rolling down the streets.

"Hello?" Meilin called, as she turned in place. "Anyone home?"

Meilin heard the creak of a door to her left. She turned and saw a pair of eyes peering through the crack.

"Excuse me..." Meilin called. But the face quickly disappeared. The wooden door of the small house slammed shut and Meilin heard the sound of a deadbolt being thrown.

Similar noises followed: more doors, opening slightly, or windows being cracked—all to be tightly snapped shut when she turned in their direction.

"Hmph!" Meilin thought. *"Friendly bunch..."* But then she reasoned, *"But it is dark, and I did fly in on a cloud—probably not what people around here are used to seeing..."*

"Hello, I'm just passing through," Meilin called out. "Just need some directions and I'll be on my way... Hello? Anyone?"

No reply.

Meilin sighed heavily. "Great..."

Meilin was about to conjure her flying cloud so she could leave when she heard another door—this one from the nearby village inn, creak open slightly.

The hushed voice of a man called out, "Hey, you! Girl! Get off the street! Hide—before *IT* gets you!"

"Before *what* gets me?"

"*IT!*"

"Ooo-kay," Meilin drawled slowly. She didn't know what an *IT* was—but by the level of fear and urgency Meilin detected in the man's voice, whatever *IT* was, *IT* didn't sound good.

"What's an *IT?*" she called, also using a hushed voice.

The man didn't answer.

Then Meilin heard a scream—a terrible scream—a mother's scream. It came from the far end of the village. It was followed by the loud crash of a wooden wall being splintered and torn apart.

Meilin spun in place and instantly morphed into her demon monkey-state. Her longest jade hair stick flew from her ponytail knot into her hand and changed to full bo staff size.

A large dark shape with many legs, much like some kind of a hideous giant black spider, scurried from a house on the perimeter of the village. In its arms was a child—a little girl no more than five years old.

The child's mother ran after the monstrous spider, wailing and pleading for her daughter's release. Her husband came crying after her, trying to restrain her from following, lest she be taken, too.

Doors quickly opened and villagers poured onto the street in confused despair.

The spider leapt up onto the roofs of the houses and hurried across them toward the darkness of the mountain.

"What the devil!" Meilin cried as she snapped into action. She jumped up to the rooftops and raced across the loose bamboo roof tiles after the fleeing creature.

The spider sensed Meilin's pursuit and sprayed sticky spider silk behind her to keep Meilin at bay.

Meilin easily dodged the spider's silk as she raced after it. She could see the terrified little girl in the spider's arms as it leapt from the rooftops into the forest.

Meilin launched herself off the rooftops, hot on the monster's tail.

The giant spider raced toward the mountain through the two kilometers of dense bamboo forest that surrounded the mountain's base.

Meilin followed close behind.

The spider, for all its size, was fast.

Meilin jumped and took to the bamboo canopy where she could leap monkey-style and pick up speed.

As she narrowed the gap from above, the spider emerged from the bamboo forest and quickly scrambled up the mountain rocks.

Meilin catapulted herself off the canopy toward the mountainside in an effort to cut the monster off from above. The giant spider reared in place, ready to meet Meilin.

Meilin was momentarily shocked when she saw the spider's face. It was the disfigured face of a woman—a demon woman!

The demon hissed at Meilin and sprayed thick spider venom from her fanged-mouth. Meilin dodged among the rocks for protection. She then vaulted up, swinging her jade bo staff at the spider demon's head.

The spider demon blocked the blow with two of its many arms. The blow from Meilin's bo rocked it—Meilin knew it did—but it was not enough to make the demon drop the child.

The spider demon spewed its sticky webbing at Meilin again. Again Meilin dodged, giving the spider demon a chance to flee across the rocky mountain face.

Meilin quickly followed.

The spider demon was adept at scurrying across the vertical face of the mountain.

Meilin wasn't.

Meilin knew that if she didn't think of something quick, she'd lose the spider—and the child.

The spider demon was on a straight path toward what looked like a jagged opening in an upper mountainside ledge.

"A cave!" Meilin surmised. If the demon made it to the opening, she could disappear inside and become impossible to find. There was no telling how deep and convoluted such a cave might be.

The child's life depended on Meilin doing something and doing it now! She had to reach the mouth of the cave first and cut the spider demon off.

Meilin leapt into the air and morphed herself into a tiny bat. With a bat's ability to fly and echolocate in the dark, Meilin was able to streak up the cliff, avoiding every obstacle the mountain had to offer.

Meilin reached the mouth of the demon spider's cave mere seconds before the spider did. She morphed back into her demon monkey-state ready for action.

Action is what she got. The spider demon somehow sensed Meilin's presence and gained the mouth of the cave ready to fight. Deadly spider venom and webbing spewed from her mouth and spinnerets at Meilin. Meilin ducked and slipped underneath the spider demon's body, ramming her jade bo staff into its abdomen. The spider demon reared up on her hind legs, trying to stab Meilin with her stinger.

Meilin parried the jabs of the stinger and swept the spider's legs out from under it with her staff. The spider demon fell onto her back, dropping the child.

Meilin spun and brought down her bo in a mighty blow.

At the same time, another figure entered the fray—an unkempt shaggy-haired man, about 30 years old, armed and wielding a Chinese long sword. He bumped into Meilin causing her to miss crushing the spider demon.

"Watch it!" he cried, as he himself tried to slash at the spider demon. But the momentary interruption was all the time the spider demon needed to make its escape and disappear into the safety of its cave.

"You stupid girl!" the man roared, clearly angry with Meilin. "Do you know how long it took me to set up this trap!"

But, Meilin wasn't listening to him. Instead, she knelt as she morphed back into her human form and gathered the frightened little girl into her arms and held her close.

The little girl melted in Meilin's arms, sobbing uncontrollably with relief, crying for her mother.

"Hey! I'm talking to you!" the man shouted again. He thrust out his fingers to poke Meilin in her shoulder to get her attention.

Meilin, angry by his intervention and his lack of concern for the little girl's condition, easily intercepted his arm, slipped underneath it, applied a wristlock, redirected his momentum and sent him flying hard onto the rocky ground.

"Oh, you're in trouble now!" he growled, staring up at her. "Just you wait! When the village elder hears about this..."

But that's not the way it went down.

The little girl Meilin saved from the spider demon was Pei, the village elder's granddaughter. He and the rest of the villagers were exceedingly grateful to Meilin for doing what the demon hunter they hired to protect the town, a man named Gao—could not.

It was now dawn and Meilin was sitting at an outside wooden table in the small courtyard of the village inn. The portly innkeeper set a steaming bowl of noodle soup on the table in front of the hungry teen.

Sitting across from Meilin was the village elder, a thin, near-toothless man named Wu. Judging by his wrinkled brow and scraggly grey hair, Meilin guessed he was in his late eighties. The rest of the small village was gathered around and watched intently.

"Please, enjoy," elder Wu said. "We're forever in your debt. Whatever reward our meager village can offer is yours."

Meilin could see by their nods and expressions that the rest of the village folk were in total agreement.

"With all due respect, elder Wu, I just need some directions," Meilin said with a smile as she deftly picked up and twirled a pair of wooden chopsticks from the table with her fingers. She then poked them into the bowl of noodles and lifted the steaming goodness to her mouth.

Elder Wu quickly signaled the innkeeper to bring more noodles to the table.

"Really," Meilin objected kindly. "One bowl is more than enough, thanks."

The smiling innkeeper placed the bowl in front of Meilin anyway and bowed repeatedly as he backed away.

"So..." Meilin said, flattered with the man's effort to please as she took another mouthful of noodles, "Anyone here know the way to Five Elements Mountain?"

Silence.

"Anyone?" Meilin stated again, scanning the watchful faces of the villagers.

Still no answer.

Meilin regarded the crowd. Their eyes were curiously blank, in spite of their smiles.

"It's kind'a like five chubby fingers sticking out of the ground," Meilin explained, holding up her left hand and spreading her fingers. "Really huge. Rising right up to the clouds."

Still, no one spoke.

"Surely you've heard of it..." Meilin remarked.

"Even if they knew, they wouldn't tell ya," a gruff voice interrupted. It was Gao.

The surly demon hunter sauntered over, pulled out a stool and sat heavily down at Meilin's table.

Meilin turned her head and stared at him.

"They're not gonna tell ya 'cause they're nothin' but a bunch'a scared rabbits who think *you* can rid them of the demon they hired me to kill! Ain't that right?" he directed to the assembled crowd.

Meilin's eyes narrowed. She didn't like Gao, or his rude way.

Meilin turned her attention back to elder Wu. She could see by his and the rest of the villagers' averted eyes, that what Gao said was true.

Meilin exhaled with disappointment and set her chopsticks down on the table.

"I see," she said, rising. "Well then, I guess I'll be on my way. Got a lot of ground to cover. Thanks for the breakfast..."

Before Meilin even finished her thought, the village elder and the entire assembly went to their knees and kowtowed.

"Immortal daughter, please don't leave us," elder Wu pleaded. "We need you. We'll do anything for you. Give you anything. You must help us. I beg you!"

"Well, first I'm not an Immortal—and secondly, I'm certainly not a demon hunter," Meilin protested.

"You are *now!*" Gao grunted as he stood. "'Cause I quit. *You* get their kids back for them!"

The gruff demon hunter turned and began to walk away.

"Hey! Wait!" Meilin called after him. "What kids? What're you talking about!"

"The ones the demon took! Ask Wu. He'll tell ya," Gao spat. He then laughed. "Or did ya think that kid ya saved last night was the only one!"

Chapter 6

"Every thirty years, just before New Year's, the spider demon comes and takes seven children," elder Wu explained. He and Meilin were now sitting in the privacy of his own modest home, located across the village square, opposite the inn. As he spoke, he cradled his exhausted sleeping granddaughter in his lap. Meilin could see nothing but love in Wu's eyes for little Pei.

"Elder," Meilin said respectfully. "How many years has this been going on?"

"Over nine hundred," Wu replied heavily.

Wu's daughter, Pei's mother, entered the room and approached with tea. Meilin waved her off. She wasn't thirsty.

The grateful young woman placed a cup in front of Meilin anyway and took her place behind her father.

"Oh my God," Meilin gasped with surprise. "Seven children every thirty years—that's...

"Two hundred and ten children," elder Wu finished for her.

The number was unsettling.

"And no one can do anything about it?"

Wu shook his head. "Our village has hired countless demon hunters over time," Wu said, motioning with his hand toward the open window of his house where Gao could be seen in the distance, sitting on the corner of a low wooden watering trough located in front of the village inn, consuming a gourd of rice wine as if he hadn't a care in the world.

"But they've all failed," he continued. He then snorted, "Or, they've all been killed. Certainly, none have ever returned to collect their payment."

Meilin shook her head with regret. "Elder," she began, "I wish I could stay and help you deal with the spider demon. But I can't. I have a mission of my own to complete and little or no time to do it. I must get to Cloud Mountain Monastery and learn the Way of the Healing Hand. A life depends on it."

Wu nodded his aged head. "I understand," he stated with regret. "The life of a friend is as valuable as the lives of our children. I just wish something could be done to save them, too."

"You mean they're still alive?" Meilin spat. She thought for sure that the taken children must already be dead.

"I believe so," Wu replied heavily. "Legend says that the spider demon only consumes the children on New Year's Eve, thus insuring her immortality, as well as maintaining her power over the Mountain Deity."

"Mountain Deity?"

"Yes. Were he free, none of this would be happening. He could tell you how to get to Five Elements Mountain. And most certainly, he could teach you the Way of the Healing Hand. But his presence hasn't been felt for over 900 years either. Still, we pray to him."

Meilin's mind raced. *'The missing children might still be alive!'* That meant she couldn't leave—her Tao wouldn't allow it. And, the spider demon wasn't immortal, Meilin was certain of that. The blows she delivered with her magical jade bo damaged the demon. If not for Gao's untimely interference, Meilin might have vanquished it and possibly freed the missing children from its lair.

"Pei was..." Meilin began.

"The seventh," Wu finished.

"Then the spider will be back."

Wu nodded gravely.

"Then it's settled. I'll stay," Meilin declared. "And put an end to this once and for all."

- - - - - - - - - - - - -

"So, let me guess... Ya took the job. *You're* their demon hunter now," Gao grunted.

"Hardly," Meilin said, confronting the man, who still seemed content with drinking his wine. "But I *will do* what I can to save the missing children."

"Well, good luck with that," Gao said standing and casting his empty wine gourd aside. "You're gonna need it."

Gao began walking toward the inn. "As for me... I'm gonna pack my stuff and be on my way. I'll be glad to get out of this rundown excuse for a village anyway."

Meilin trailed after him.

"How can you leave? Those missing children might still be alive!"

"Maybe. Maybe not." Gao said flatly. "Not my problem anymore."

Meilin grabbed Gao by the arm and stopped him.

"What kind of demon hunter are you!" she demanded.

"A live one!" Gao replied, tugging his arm free from Meilin's grasp. "And if ya want my advice, you'd leave, too! Those fancy Kung fu moves of yours ain't gonna do ya any good next time. That spider ain't stupid. Though I do wonder how ya managed to scale the mountainside so quickly."

Gao paused and studied Meilin closely. It was dark when they first met and he didn't fully see her in her demon monkey form. "You ain't quite human, are ya! Where you from, girl? And don't gimme that line ya handed Wu that you're just passin' through..."

"I'm from Shuilian-dong," Meilin replied.

"Hmph!" Gao snorted. "That's monkey country. You don't look monkey to me."

"I'm also half fae," Meiln stated.

Gao tilted his head. "Huh! Now ain't that somethin'. Half fae. Got some magic in ya—do ya?"

Gao continued to study Meilin closely. "Yeah, you got some magic..."

Gao then smiled. "Alright, tell ya what. You can work with me. But ya do exactly as I say. And we split the money 70-30. Got it? It's only fair. I did all the groundwork before ya even got here!"

"But I don't want your help," Meilin stated, confused by Gao's sudden turnaround. "And I certainly don't want the money."

"Ha!" Gao snorted. "You wanna save those kids, don't ya?"

"Yes..."

"And I suppose ya been inside the spider demon's cave like I have?"

"No, but..."

"Then it's settled," Gao replied. "We'll meet at dusk, right here. Till then, I suggest ya get some food and some sleep. It's gonna be a long night."

Gao then spun on his heels and headed inside the inn, leaving Meilin to wonder how someone so obviously despicable just ended up taking over her mission.

Chapter 7

Meilin didn't take Gao's advice about the sleep or the food. She wasn't tired and she wasn't hungry. Instead, she used the time to find a quiet place under a shady tree on a knoll at the edge of the village to think about her friend Jessie, Jessie's grandmother, her own mother and Uncle Z.

It was beyond doubt that her mother and uncle were furious with her for using the Gate without permission and when this whole thing was said and done, she knew she'd probably be grounded for life—or worse. But it couldn't be helped. Meilin fully disagreed with her mother's decision not to help Jessie's grandmother because, in her uncle's words, *"it was against the Tao."* She didn't buy that at all.

What good was understanding the nature of the Tao if you couldn't use it to help people?

Jessie's grandmother was dying and if Meilin was in a position to do something, wasn't that the right thing to do?

Of course it was! It had to be!

What other conclusion could one reach? Besides, Meilin made a promise to help Jessie. Jessie was more than her BFF—she was like her sister and Meilin would do no less. Meilin needed to be proactive and take the helm.

"An ant on the move does more than a dozing ox!" her Uncle Z once told her—another of old Lao's fortune-cookie sayings.

So it was up to her to take this on, learn the Way of the Healing Hand and save Jessie's grandmother.

But in order to do any of that, Meilin first had to defeat the spider demon and rescue the missing children. That took priority over everything.

Meilin prayed that elder Wu's story, that the spider demon only consumed her prey on New Year's Eve, was true. If it was, then the children were still alive and had a chance. If it wasn't, then Meilin vowed that she would at least put an end to the horror that plagued the village for over 900 years. She couldn't imagine the pain and grief the parents of all those missing children must have suffered over the centuries.

Meilin also wondered what kind of demon the spider really was. Was it intelligent? Was it evil? Was it acting out of instinct? If it was, then it wasn't necessarily malevolent. Or did it, like so many demons, simply hate humans?

Too many questions.

If only Uncle Z were here to shed his insight on the matter of demons. Both Zhu and her father once had to contend with spider demons—sisters, Meilin recalled, who appeared as beautiful women to entice travelers and then lure them to their web of death.

But this spider demon wasn't beautiful and didn't entice wayward travelers. She came in the dead of night and stole children—a far different kind of demon, indeed.

Meilin shifted her back against her tree and gazed out across the fields.

She then saw a curious sight. A column of women and a group of small children, Pei and her mother among them, walking single file out of the village. They were all dressed in white. The women carried long smoldering joss sticks. The children bore flowers. One woman struck a small brass gong as they walked.

"A funeral procession?" Meilin wondered. She took to her feet and hastened to follow.

Meilin caught up to the women and children as they entered a clearing, just beyond the far edge of the bamboo forest line.

The clearing was a graveyard, lined with several rows of gravestones. The granite markers were about three feet tall and twelve inches wide. Each was engraved with a name. Meilin could also tell by their close proximity, that no bodies were buried beneath them. No one dared go into the spider's cave to retrieve any remains.

"These are the names of all our taken children," Pei's mother said solemnly as Meilin joined the group. They wove their way slowly past every marker, careful not to miss any. "We honor them every year."

The group finally stopped before seven new markers that were planted in the ground.

"And these are the markers for our seven children who've been taken this year." The women then raised their joss sticks to their heads and began their prayers. Tears flowed freely down their faces and Meilin understood that these were the mothers of the missing children.

All the names were there, including little Pei's. In spite of the fact that Meilin had saved her, the women were resigned to the inevitable: that the spider demon would come and take her again.

Then Meilin's eyes widened.

There weren't seven new markers planted in the ground. There were eight.

The eighth marker bore the name—Meilin.

Chapter 8

"We meant no disrespect," Pei's mother later explained to Meilin after the ceremony to honor the missing children was over. The twenty-six-year-old modest-looking woman had a pleasant, though somewhat lined, face—the result, Meilin suspected, of the years of dread knowing that her child was growing up in the midst of the spider demon's thirty-year cycle of death.

Her name was Chun. She and the other mothers asked Meilin to sit with them for awhile in the graveyard to talk.

Little Pei, still tired from her harrowing ordeal and now the long honoring ceremony, came over to Meilin and sat in her lap. Meilin smiled and cuddled the little girl close. Pei returned Meilin's affection and melted into her embrace. As Meilin held Pei in her arms, Pei reached up and played with the jade Monkey King pendent that hung from Meilin's neck. The polished stone glittered in the sunlight.

"You like that?" Meilin asked softly.

Pei shook her head, yes.

Meilin smiled again, reached around to the back of her neck with her free hand and undid the tiny silver clasp that joined the ends of the thin black silk cord together.

"Then it's yours," Meilin said, handing it to Pei. "I want you to have it. Something to remember me by."

"No, we couldn't," Chun protested.

"Of course you can," Meilin countered. "Besides, Pei and I are sisters now. Isn't that right?" she said with a wink.

Pei smiled her biggest smile as Meilin fastened the necklace around the little girl's neck.

"It looks beautiful on you," Meilin said, giving her another loving hug. Pei beamed with joy.

"Meilin, we know you mean well," Chun began. "And you want to help save our children. But, if you wish to leave, no one here will think less of you for going."

"I'm not going anywhere," Meilin said.

"Never mind what you promised my father," Chun returned. "The men in our village don't have to live with it as *we* do."

"The spider demon can't be defeated," the grieving mother named Fan added. "We accept the fact that our children are lost."

"We don't want you to sacrifice yourself for something you can't achieve," the mother named Yue stated flatly.

"Yes, but..."

"Meilin—by your own admission, you're not immortal," Chun said. "Therefore, what can you do that so many others couldn't? You're only a child yourself..."

"Well," Meilin replied with a degree of confidence, "I hope I'm a bit more than a child... And you're right, I'm far from immortal—but, I do know a few tricks."

Chung slowly shook her head. "There's another graveyard near here," she cited, "with markers bearing the names of demon hunters who've also never returned. All were capable men skilled in fighting. All of them proclaimed to know *tricks*..."

"Is your mother still alive?" Yue asked.

"Yes, of course," Meilin answered.

"Then go home," Chun begged. "We don't want her to grieve as *we* do. A mother should never have to grieve for her child."

Meilin studied each of the women's faces. She could see in their tired eyes that they were desperately serious. None of them wanted Meilin to sacrifice her life for a cause that they believed to be hopeless.

And there was one more thing besides the hopelessness Meilin saw in their eyes.

Resignation.

The cycle of death had gone on in their village for so long that each had grown up resigned to their probable fate as mothers. This was what disturbed Meilin the most. The mothers of the village had already given up even before their children were born. The spider demon had wrought more than death upon the inhabitants of this poor community. It had also killed their spirit.

Meilin thought of telling Chun and the women who she really was—Meilin, daughter of Sun Wukong the Monkey King—and that she likely had the power to defeat any demon that crossed her path, though her powers and abilities had not yet fully manifested or been tested.

But that would be bragging—and decidedly untrue. She had been lucky thus far in her journey of self-discovery. Extraordinarily lucky. Besides, the women were right. Meilin wasn't immortal. And Meilin knew herself that she wasn't undefeatable. Her cantankerous martial arts instructor, Taoist Master Zhao, could easily defeat her during training. No, Meilin knew she still had a lot to learn about herself and it would take her a lifetime to learn it.

Meilin clasped her hands together and bowed her head before the assembled mothers.

"Thank you for your concern and I grieve for your losses," Meilin said reverently. "But I assure you, I won't leave until this demon is vanquished and your children are returned."

The mothers bowed their heads in kind to Meilin.

"If we can't dissuade you..." Chun said.

"You can help me," Meilin suggested.

"How?"

"By telling me more about the spider demon," Meilin said. "When did the killings start? Why did they start? And what about Mountain Deity? You still pray to him. Has he ever answered *any* of your prayers?"

The women looked at each other with surprise—and, Meilin detected, a very, very small glint of hope. They could see that Meilin was quite determined to do as she said.

"A long time ago," Chun began, "our village was prosperous and our rice harvest bountiful—not like it is today. Mountain Deity was generous. Water from the mountain streams irrigated our fields and maintained our livestock. We had enough to eat and sustain us through the winters. When people were sick, we went to his shrine and prayed for his help. Usually our prayers were answered. The healing powers of our mountain were so legendary, people would travel great distances to pray—even kings. Then one year, the mountain streams stopped flowing, our crops failed, and our town fell into misery. It was during that year that the spider demon first appeared and began to take our children. We prayed to Mountain Deity to help us, but our prayers went unanswered. Mountain Deity had abandoned us, for reasons we've yet to understand. The spider demon continues to come, and we are as you see us now, defeated, barely hanging on, hoping that one day our misery will end and our lives—the lives of our children, will be restored."

Meilin nodded slowly as she digested their story. What was once an idyllic life was shattered with the sudden appearance of the spider demon. So, where did it come from and why? Demon-kind were commonplace in this era and still shared the world with humans, even if contentiously. This, Meilin knew, would ultimately change and the balance of power would shift in favor of humankind. But that was the future, not the here and now. Meilin also knew that the dominion of humankind would likely not last forever either.

The balance of power would ultimately shift again—perhaps sooner than expected, especially with the precarious path that modern mankind seemed to be on. *"Nature is not human-hearted,"* she remembered Zhu Bajie saying.

"Chun," Meilin asked out of curiosity, "When all of this first began, why didn't your ancestors simply move on? Find another place to live?"

"Where?" Chun answered. "Where could they go? This is our home—our land. Where could they go that the spider demon wouldn't follow? Where could they go that others wouldn't turn them away, in fear that the demon spider would attack them too? We're a cursed people and we know it."

Meilin sighed heavily with Chun's ingrained resignation. *"Fate's net is vast and its mesh coarse, yet none escape it,"* her Uncle Zhu once told her during one of his many lessons about the Tao. *"It does not ask, yet all things answer to it. It does not call, yet all things meet it. It does not plan, yet all things are determined by it."*

This was true. Fate would happen, no matter what. But he also said that Fate and Destiny were *not* the same. Destiny was something one could either *let* happen to them—or *make* happen. The people of this village had confused their fate with their destiny.

Meilin knew from her lessons that everyone

and everything was part of the fabric of the Tao. The Tao flowed like water, through and around everything. That meant that one's own Tao, like flowing water, could be channeled to flow in the direction one needed.

"If you don't change direction, you may end up where you're heading," her uncle also once said during a lesson. That, at least, was one of old Lao's teachings that didn't need to be explained. But the problem was, people often didn't know the direction they were heading because they were too caught up in the immediate minutia of the path they were taking.

If the villagers were incapable of changing the direction of their destiny, Meilin was resolved to change it *for* them—if she could.

Meilin lifted the now dozing Pei across to her mother's arms and then stood.

"Thank you," she said, smiling at the women. "I appreciate your counsel. Now, if you'd be so kind as to tell me where Mountain Deity's shrine is, I'd like to see it before it gets dark." Meilin paused, then added, "Oh—and one more thing..."

Chapter 9

Meilin found Mountain Deity's shrine exactly where the women said it would be—halfway up the rocky mountain trail at the back of a small flat clearing, about 600 yards below the mouth of the spider demon's cave.

The stone shrine itself was small and typically Chinese. But rather than a bas-relief of Mountain Deity carved into the surrounding basalt and granite, this shrine had instead a freestanding four-foot-tall solid stone effigy of the mountain god.

The villagers who still dared to journey up the mountain to worship here—in spite of Mountain Deity's 900-year absence—meticulously kept the shrine free of leaves, roots and other debris.

"At least they still have their faith," Meilin thought, though little of even that was left.

At the base of the shrine was a small stone basin that Meilin could tell was once fed by a mountain spring that trickled through a thin crack in the surrounding rocks.

Water from this spring, Chun had said, was reputed to have healing properties that could cure any disease. Whether or not that was really true, Meilin couldn't say. But it was enough that the villagers believed it did. Meilin knew that water blessed by a deity could do amazing things.

But Meilin could also tell that water from this mountain spring hadn't flowed through the crack in the rocks for a very long time. Centuries, she reasoned, by the weathering of the surrounding stone.

Meilin approached the effigy of Mountain Deity for a closer look. The carving was that of a kind-looking old man, rather sage-like in appearance with a waist-long beard. His left hand was positioned in a lotus gesture, very much like a Buddha's. His right hand was at his waist, palm upward, as if he once had cradled something in it—a polished stone, or perhaps even a large crystal. Whatever it once was, it was long missing.

At the Mountain Deity's feet were two small carved stone bowls. There were a few grains of rice still in one that the birds had yet to find. They were offering bowls, Meilin knew, that worshipers used as a gesture of their appreciation for the deity's favor. In an affluent society, money would be placed in the bowls. But here, a few grains of rice were all the poor villagers of this country community could manage.

Meilin put her palms together, went to her knees and bowed reverently to the stone effigy.

"Mountain Deity," she whispered. "Can you hear me?"

No answer.

Meilin tried again.

"Mountain Deity, I've come to ask your help in saving the missing children from the village below. If you can hear me—can you help me? Please? On behalf of their mothers, I beg you... I need your guidance."

Still, no answer.

Meilin frowned. Of course there was no answer. Meilin expected as much. Why should her plea result in anything different from anyone else's? It's been 900 years.

Still, Meilin was no ordinary pilgrim. She was the daughter of Sun Wukong, the Monkey King. That meant she had the power to summon an earth-bound deity the same way her father could—and had done so many times during his fabled *Journey to the West*.

But how did he do it? That was the question.

Was it a spell? An incantation? Or did he simply will it to happen—like he could with so many of his powers and abilities?

Magic was a subject Meilin definitely knew she'd have to take up with her Uncle Z when she returned home—that is, *if* he were still talking to her. Meilin openly defied his attempt to keep her from entering the Gate. Furthermore, she'd slammed it shut and locked it right in his face.

Meilin knew she'd have to pay big-time for that one. But it was a price she was willing to pay in order to help Jessie and her grandmother. Besides, the chubby old demon pig could never stay mad at her for long. He was far too loving and forgiving for that.

Her mother, on the other hand... That was bound to be a different situation. Meilin had to face the fact that *"grounded for life"* would be the least punishment she could hope for. Yet, Meilin had defied her mother once before—when she flew off to confront the demon, Hong Hái-Er, on Fire Mountain. Lijuan was furious with Meilin when she returned. Yet, she also accepted the fact that Meilin had to follow her own Tao and confront Red Boy in order to stop him from destroying Shuilian-dong in his insane quest to take revenge on everyone and everything connected to her father.

Meilin fought for her father's kingdom that day—and for her kin. But this time, she'd defied her mother to help *one* person, a dying woman she didn't even know, who, her mother said, could not be saved.

And now, here Meilin was, kneeling on a mountainside, wondering if and how she could summon an ancient deity to somehow help save six more lives—innocent children, to boot!

To further complicate matters, Meilin knew she was running out of time. Jessie's grandmother would soon be dead, in spite of all the modern medical technology her doctors employed to keep her alive.

Worse, tomorrow was New Year's Day, which meant that tonight was New Year's Eve—the moment when the spider demon would, according to local legend, consume the missing children.

No, Meilin knew she'd really screwed up big time. Lives counted on her doing the right thing— and here she was, clueless, unable to manage even a simple summons.

Meilin now knew that in spite of her good intentions, she was cocky and arrogant in her reasoning and therefore out of balance with her Tao. She'd been so sure that because she was the Monkey King's daughter, she could automatically accomplish anything. And here she was, on the verge of accomplishing nothing.

"Accomplish without boasting. Accomplish without show. Accomplish without arrogance..." More of Zhu Bajie's pronouncements echoed in her head. If only Zhu were here now...

Meilin's monkey senses piqued. Someone or something was approaching.

It was Gao.

"Heard you were up here. Prayin' to that dumb old statue ain't gonna help ya," he grunted as he entered the rocky clearing to the shrine.

"How do *you* know?" Meilin returned.

"'Cause it's a rock! Ain't nothin' magical ever come from a rock," he snorted.

Meilin wanted to object, *"Wanna bet? My father came from a rock that fell from the heavens—and he's pretty darn magical!"*

But she didn't. She kept her mouth closed.

The grungy demon hunter came to Meilin's side where she still knelt. Meilin's nostrils flared. Gao stunk of rice wine and she could tell that the unkempt man hadn't bathed for a long while— years, maybe.

"It's just a hunk'a rock somebody carved up a long time ago," he continued. "Useless. Just like believin' in Mountain Deity is useless!"

Meilin stood and faced Gao. He was a full foot taller than Meilin and he gazed down at her with a disdainful look in his eyes. Meilin could tell that he didn't like her.

Fine—she didn't like him either. And for a demon hunter, Gao didn't seem all that driven or skilled to do his job. But she knew she had to work with him, to save the children. He said he'd been inside the spider demon's cave. That, at least, was something that could prove useful. If the cave was as voluminous as Shuilian-dong, it could take days to ferret out the spider demon— even longer to find where she might have hidden the missing children.

"Stupid superstition!" Gao growled as he raised his leg to kick the statue over.

"Don't!" Meilin ordered, swiftly stepping directly in front of him, shielding the statue of Mountain Deity with her body. She steeled herself to deflect the thrust of his kick.

"Just because *you* don't believe..." Meilin asserted.

"Hmph!" Gao snorted, measuring Meilin's determination to protect the effigy. He slowly lowered his leg. "You know this thing's kept these people prisoner as much as that spider demon has!"

"Or, maybe it's their *faith* in it that's kept them going," Meilin countered.

Gao laughed with disdain. "You some kind'a priest as well as a demon hunter?"

"No," Meilin answered. "I'm not a priest. I'm just someone who wants to help save some missing children. And if you were any kind of man—you'd want to do the same."

"You don't know what kind of man I am or what I've been through, missy! So don't you lecture me—about *anything!*"

Gao was right about that. Meilin didn't know anything about him—where he was from, or how or why he came to be here. But from where she was standing, Meilin knew she didn't want to.

Meilin could also see that Gao wasn't simply some drifter who'd taken up demon hunting just to get by. He was a very *angry* man with deep-rooted resentment for nearly everyone and everything that crossed his path.

In some way, Meilin felt sorry for him. Gao was definitely out of balance with his Tao. But Meilin also knew that she wasn't a psychologist or an enlightened sage with the skills to guide him back to his center. She was still learning how to keep her own mind centered and in balance with her own Tao. Luckily, she had her uncle Zhu Bajie, her mother and countless others to help her. Gao, apparently, had no one.

"It's easier to carry an empty cup, than one filled to the brim," Meilin offered. If Gao could empty himself of his problems, maybe...

"Save your breath! That Taoist rubbish don't mean nothin' to me," Gao snorted as he turned his back on Meilin and began walking away.

After a few steps, he stopped.

"Well? You comin'?" he said with annoyance. "Spider demons don't kill themselves, ya know!"

Chapter 10

It was dusk when Meilin and Gao gained the narrow ledge at the mouth of the spider demon's cave.

The two made the long trek up the winding mountain trail in relative silence. Well, relative silence for one of them, anyway.

Gao had nothing to say or offer as to what they might expect when they encountered the demon. He either snorted or grunted at every question Meilin posed. She couldn't tell if any of the guttural noises the sour man made meant either 'yes' or 'no.'

"You talk a lot!" Gao complained. "Anyone ever tell you that?"

"No," Meilin replied with a shrug. "Quite the opposite, in fact."

"Hmph!" Gao snorted again and grumbled, "Lucky me, then."

"I just wanna know what you really think we're up against," Meilin said.

"We're up against a really big spider," Gao snapped. "Or have you forgotten already!"

"I haven't forgotten," Meilin answered. She well knew what she was up against—and what she had to do. The problem was, Meilin knew deep inside that she really didn't want to kill the spider demon—no matter how evil it might be. At least, she didn't want to kill it until she understood what it was all about. That was against her Tao.

"Give evil nothing to oppose, and it will disappear," Zhu Bajie once told her. If Meilin could find out why the spider demon was doing what it did, then maybe there was a solution other than simply killing it.

Maybe.

Maybe not.

In the end, the lives of the village children came first. *That*, Meilin knew, was an absolute.

Meilin stepped to the edge of the precipice they were on and peered down at the village, thousands of feet below.

"I wouldn't stand too close," Gao advised. "It's a long way down. Hate for you to fall."

"That's okay," Meilin replied. "Heights don't bother me." And they didn't. Meilin used to be afraid of heights—and just about everything else.

But all of her fears and inhibitions began to dissipate after her fourteenth birthday—when her demon monkey powers began to manifest and she discovered who she really was.

"What'ya lookin' at anyway?" Gao asked, joining her.

"The village," Meilin remarked casually.

"What about it?"

"Just making sure everyone left."

"They what!"

"I told everyone to gather their children and leave," Meilin said with a smile. "Just a precaution, you know—in case something goes wrong."

Gao's jaw tightened. "You told everyone to leave?" he restated. "By whose authority?"

"Mine," Meilin answered. "No reason to put anyone at risk—especially since the spider demon needs a seventh victim. Right?"

Meilin studied Gao. His eyes were dark and cold. But his face smiled.

"Yeah. Good thinkin'," he said begrudgingly. "Should'a thought of that myself."

"Didn't think you'd mind," Meilin continued. "Once New Year's Eve passes, it's all over anyway. Nothing the spider demon can do then, right? Well, at least not for another 30 years..."

"Yeah..." Gao mouthed. "Not for another 30 years."

Meilin smiled. "At first I thought, '*Meilin, maybe you should check with Gao.*' But then I thought, '*Nah, he's busy,* so *why bother him with it?*' Besides, it seemed so obvious."

Gao closed his eyes and shook his head.

"Look—can you just stop talking?" he muttered. "You're givin' me a headache."

"Oh... Sorry," Meilin said apologetically. She then gazed into the mouth of the cave. "It's pretty dark in there. We should've brought some torches."

Gao grunted again. "Way ahead of ya."

Gao turned and walked over to the mouth of the cave, knelt to the ground and fished something out of the dirt. It looked like twine, the kind Meilin's mother Lijuan used to secure the paper packages of medicinal herbs she measured out for her customers in her apothecary located in the basement of Zhu Bajie's shop. Gao tugged its length free and Meilin could see that it ran deep into the cave.

Gao then fished a piece of flint from his pocket and struck it against the dagger he pulled from his belt. The brown twine immediately caught fire.

It was a fuse. Instantly, the fire ran down the length of the thin cord.

"Hey!" Meilin exclaimed anxiously. "You're not gonna blow the place up, are ya?"

"Watch and learn, girlie," Gao growled. Within seconds, the burning fuse made its way to several small red paper lanterns hung at various intervals throughout the beginnings of the cave. Soon, parts of the cavern began to light up with a faint amber and crimson glow.

"Cool!" Meilin remarked, joining Gao.

It was pretty creepy, too!

The cave was long, narrow and convoluted, not voluminous like Shuilian-dong. Meilin imagined that there were plenty of tunnels leading off to all sides—any one of which the spider demon could be hiding in, waiting to pounce. Thick spider silk lined and hung from the cave's walls everywhere. That, coupled with the eerie shadows Gao's lanterns created, made the cave feel even more deadly.

Gao grinned. "Told ya I've been in the cave before. Not so dumb after all, am I!"

Meilin nodded. In truth, Meilin never thought Gao was dumb. In fact, she didn't know what to make of him at all. And the lantern idea was a good one—though Meilin didn't need their light. She could see perfectly well in the dark, just like her father could. But she kept that fact to herself.

Gao then drew his Chinese longsword from its scabbard. He spun its sharp blade about his body a few times, testing the measure of its balance in his right hand.

"Guess we better get to it then," he said.

Meilin nodded and took a step toward the cave.

Gao's arm stayed her.

"Where's your weapon?" Gao demanded. "Or you just figurin' on *talkin'* the spider demon to death!"

"No..." Meilin said with a touch of self-consciousness, wondering, *"Do I really talk too much?"*

"Oh, yeah, I forgot," Gao said, continuing with his slight. "You're a Kung fu *master.*"

"Hardly," Meilin admitted. "But, I *am* taking lessons," she said with a confident smile.

Gao shook his head with disgust. "Here," he said, pulling the dagger he'd just used to strike the flint with from his belt.

"Take this," he grunted.

"No thanks," Meilin said. "Don't like sharp pointy things."

Gao stared at Meilin for a long second then snorted. "Suit yourself," he said, replacing the dagger in his belt. "Just don't come cryin' to me when the spider demon's breathin' down your neck."

Gao then brushed roughly past her, taking the lead. Meilin fell in step behind him.

After walking about one hundred feet into the interior of the cave, Meilin suddenly asked, "Gao, how did you get this job?"

"You're talkin' again!" Gao growled with annoyance.

"Sorry," Meilin replied. "It's just—the village is really in the middle of nowhere," Meilin continued. "It's not like they had posters up advertising for a demon hunter. How'd you learn about the job?"

"I stumbled across it. Same as you."

"Yeah, but…"

Gao halted in his tracks and turned. "Look!" he growled, "Are we sneakin' up on a demon here, or playin' twenty questions!"

"Well, actually," Meilin said with certainty, "With all these lanterns lit up, I'm pretty sure the spider demon knows we're here. So, the more likely scenario is that it's gonna sneak up on *us*."

"Well, ain't we the clever one!"

"I'm just sayin'," Meilin remarked.

"Well don't!" Gao barked. "You come in here, wreck my trap—take my job—and now you're drivin' me nuts with your constant blabber! It's like you're makin' all this noise 'cause you want the spider demon to come. If you're in such a hurry to die, go ahead," Gao said, gesturing deeper into the cave. "Be my guest!"

"I'm not in any hurry to die," Meilin countered. "But a little truth between us would be nice."

"What truth!" Gao snapped indignantly.

"For starters, how about telling me who you really are."

"*Who I really am?* I'm a demon hunter. Same as you."

"Well, see—that's just the thing—I'm not," Meilin countered. "The point is, you've been in this cave deep enough to hang these lanterns. That means you've been here enough times to know where the children are."

"You're really crazy! You know that!" Gao spat. "If I knew where the kids were, don't ya think I'd have brought them out?"

"Well, that's sort'a what I've been wondering," Meilin replied.

"I ain't brought the kids out 'cause I don't know where they are!" Gao hissed. "There's a lot of tunnels in here and I ain't been in them all. And if you wanna know what I really think—I think they're already dead! And if they're not—they're soon gonna be! So how about keepin' your pretty little yap shut and concentrate on gettin' this job done!"

"Touché," Meilin silently conceded. She was deliberately irritating Gao hoping to learn a bit more about his character and background, but it was clear he wasn't going to offer up any information she didn't already know.

Indeed, Gao was a very difficult man to decipher. He wasn't the sort of demon hunter Meilin imagined a demon hunter should be—a handsome knight who came to the village on a white horse, prepared to slay the monster, rescue the children and lift the curse that had plagued the mountainside for centuries.

No, Meilin had to settle on the fact that Gao was nothing more than an ordinary man—an opportunist or a drifter down on his luck, who took a job he probably knew he couldn't do just for the money, with plans of moving on whether he killed the spider demon or not. *"So much for fairytale heroes,"* Meilin thought.

"Any more questions?" Gao glowered.

Meilin shook her head, no.

"We can go on then?"

Meilin shook her head, yes.

"Good," Gao grunted. "Up ahead, the tunnel splits. I've been down the shaft to the left and there's nuthin' in it. It dead-ends after about forty yards. The tunnel on the right—that's a different story. I've only been down that one far enough to know that it splits again. So, we can either each take a tunnel—or stay together. I'm for splittin' up. Cover more ground that way."

"I think we should stay together," Meilin countered.

"Why?"

Meilin wanted to say, *"Because, like in every bad horror film ever made, when you know there's a monster in either one of two places, the heroes always split up and one always gets killed."* But that would necessitate an explanation as to what a horror film was; and Meilin knew that Gao was already not in the mood for any more of her nonsense.

"Because there's strength in numbers," Meilin said. "Besides, if we come across the missing children, we're both gonna have to be there."

Gao considered Meilin's reasoning and nodded.

"Okay," he said. "Have it your way."

Gao turned and walked over to the nearest hanging lantern he had previously positioned in the cave. He reached up with his sword and lifted the lantern down with the tip of its blade.

"We'll need this," he said.

Gao then scanned the debris scattered along the cave's floor until he found an old dried root half-covered in spider silk. It was about five feet long and fairly straight. Gao tied the lantern to one end of the root and handed it to Meilin.

Armed with a lantern to light the rest of their way, the two continued on and soon were proceeding cautiously down the tunnel that, as Gao had previously stated, forked to the right.

After another 30 yards, the tunnel split again.

"Gotta preference?" Gao said with a hushed voice.

Meilin stepped forward and gazed down both dark corridors. Using her demon monkey vision to see further than the glow their tiny lantern could manage, Meilin could tell that the path to the right narrowed considerably and seemed impassable for a creature the size of the spider demon to comfortably negotiate. The path to the left however, appeared to expand in height as if it might lead to an interior chamber.

"Let's take the path to the left," she said.

Gao shrugged and Meilin could tell by his expression that either direction didn't matter much to him. It was now less than a few hours until midnight, New Years Eve. If they didn't encounter the spider demon by then, Meilin knew Gao would probably give up, return to the village, collect his payment in the morning, and leave.

It wasn't long before Meilin's hunch proved correct. The left path opened into a fairly large cavern deep inside the mountain. Instead of the randomly-spewed spider silk that lined the tunnels, the walls inside the cavern were covered in perfectly spun webs.

"This could be it!" Meilin whispered.

"Better be careful," Gao advised, resetting his grip on his sword. The two proceeded with caution, scanning the walls in every direction, left, right—and overhead. The webs ran everywhere.

Then Meilin's heart stopped.

At the far end of the cave, Meilin spotted several child-sized web-wrapped cocoons hanging from the webbing on the cavern walls.

The children!

Meilin dropped her lantern to the ground as she spun in place, staring at all the walls and up to the web-lined ceiling. There were silk-wrapped mummies everywhere! Dozens of them! No— hundreds! Two hundred and sixteen to be exact!

"Oh—my—God!" Meilin gasped, reflexively bringing her hands to her face in an effort to shield her eyes from the horror!

"We're too late," Gao said, coming to Meilin's side.

Meilin's eyes flooded with tears and she was about to agree when she detected from the corner of her watery eyes, a tiny movement from one of the silk-wrapped mummies to her far right.

Could it be?

The small body-shaped web-cocoon was one of six suspended about four feet off the ground. The webbing was slick and looked new—not like the dust-covered webbing in the rest of the cavern.

"Look! Over there!" Meilin cried as she ran toward the cocoons. She placed her left hand on the one that moved.

It moved again.

Whatever was inside—was alive!

Meilin's demon monkey-senses suddenly tingled. It was the spider demon! She was close—very close.

Meilin's eyes scanned the walls and ceiling.

Then she saw it—the spider demon—scurrying upside-down across the cavern ceiling, heading right for them. The demon was as hideous as she remembered.

"Oh, snap! Gao!" Meilin commanded. "Quick! Cut the kids down! I'll stall her!"

"Right!" Gao said, stepping quickly behind Meilin, pulling his dagger from his belt. But instead of using it to cut the webbed-cocoons down, Gao raked his dagger along the wall, dropping a massive net of sticky spider webbing directly on top of Meilin.

The webbing was surprisingly heavy and covered with viscous spider demon venom.

"Gao! What're you doing!" Meilin cried as she struggled against the webbing. But the more Meilin struggled, the more entangled she got—and the faster the numbing venom seeped through her skin. Meilin tried to go full-monkey and change into her demon monkey-state—but she couldn't! The spider's venom had seen to that.

Instantly, the spider demon leapt from the cavern above and pounced on Meilin. The spider demon scooped Meilin up in her spidery forearms and began to rotate her, spewing spider silk from her spinnerets, wrapping Meilin up in a tight web cocoon. At the same time, the spider plunged her deadly stinger into Meilin's right thigh, delivering a massive dose of poison into her body. The pain from the stab of the stinger was excruciating.

Within seconds Meilin could feel herself losing control of her motor functions as the spider venom coursed through her veins.

Gao's maniacal laughter filled Meilin's ears, as she lay helpless, unable to move.

"Take her, my love! She's fae!" Meilin could hear Gao cry joyously. "She's fae! She's fae! Our 900 years of waiting are over!"

It had been a set-up all along and Meilin fell for it. Gao played her perfectly. The demon hunter's trap wasn't for the spider demon—it was for her.

But, why? What was the connection between the two?

Meilin's head reeled as she fought to maintain focus. But she couldn't. She felt herself slipping away fast. There was only one thing that Meilin knew she could do to save herself—something she dreaded more than dying.

Meilin had to use shadow magic—the same dark magic she had learned from her friend, Xiao Hong, the Huli-jing she met when she first journeyed back in Time to the era of the Monkey King.

Shadow magic was magic Meilin swore to herself that she never wanted to use—ever. It ran against every fiber of her being and her Tao.

But Meilin knew she had no choice. The only way to save herself was to enter the Shadow Realm. The only way she could save herself—was by becoming a wraith.

Meilin gathered every last ounce of strength and energy she had and focused it on one thought and one thought only, *"Yang is Yin. Yin is Yang. Separate, yet inseparable. One flows into the other. Yang is Yin. Yin is Yang. Separate, yet inseparable. One flows into the other."*

Meilin felt herself slipping away.

"Yang is Yin. Yin is Yang. Separate, yet inseparable. One flows into the other. Yang is Yin. Yin is Yang..."

Just before Meilin succumbed completely to the demon spider's venom, the gateway to the Shadow Realm opened to her and she felt herself falling into its all-consuming darkness.

"No!" Gao screamed at the top of his lungs as he witnessed the body of Meilin virtually wink-out and disappear right before his eyes! *"No! No! No!"*

The spider demon, too, losing her prize, went berserk and unleashed a long, terrifying banshee-like wail that echoed throughout the cavern, resonated through the tunnels, and exited through the mouth of the cave into the stillness of the night.

Chapter 11

When Meilin regained her senses, she found herself still inside a cavern—yet, not the same cavern she had just left. This was a strange and surreal cavern with walls that pulsated and moved as if they had a life of their own.

Was she inside the depths of the living Mountain?

No. It was just one of the many ghostly manifestations of the Shadow Realm, where everything was turned upside-down—a dark, cold, foreboding and lonely place where what was real, and what was surreal, was indistinguishable.

Meilin struggled to stand. The poison was still in her and she found it difficult to move. Her entire right thigh throbbed with burning pain from the spider demon's sting.

"Argh!" she winced, placing her right hand over the stinger wound. She tried to walk, but could only manage a hobbled limp.

Again, Meilin's demon monkey-senses tingled. Was it the spider demon? Could she too, cross over into the Shadow Realm? If she could...

Meilin scanned the cavern. Something was coming—and coming fast! Her innate senses told her that whatever it was—it wasn't good!

Then Meilin saw them—a swarm of child-sized ghostly black apparitions, flying straight for her. Their razor-sharp fangs gnashed like piranhas. They had large, empty black holes where their eyes should have been; and the tips of their fingers on their tiny hands were pointed and sharp.

Meilin's instinct was to run, but she couldn't. Her leg wouldn't let her. She had to face whatever they were if she were going to survive.

Meilin's longest jade hair stick flew into her hands and instantly morphed to bo staff size. Again, she tried to change into her demon monkey-state, but couldn't. The spider venom still had control of her body.

Within seconds the swarm was on her. Meilin's bo staff flew about her, batting the biting wraiths away. Yet, for every one she hit, another took its place.

They raged around her, nipping, biting, clawing—it was all Meilin could do in her weakened state to keep them at bay.

Worse, Meilin knew she couldn't keep it up forever. Her strength was waning fast.

"This way!" an ethereal voice urgently called out! It was a woman's voice.

Meilin turned her face in the direction of the voice and saw the ghostly apparition of a young woman. Her skin was as pale as chalk. Her hair was long and black and covered much of her visage. Meilin guessed the ghost girl to be in her early twenties. She beckoned frantically for Meilin to follow her.

"Little busy here!" Meilin grunted, still straining to keep the biting dark wraiths from tearing her to shreds.

The ghostly girl floated toward Meilin, making a swirling motion with her hands. She quickly created a softball-sized orb of pale blue light between her palms that she then cast out at the raging swarm. The orb flew into their midst and erupted into a sphere of intense white light that hovered above them in the cavern, sending the menacing black wraiths cowering for the safety of darkness.

The ghost girl then grabbed Meilin by the hand and pulled her along as fast as Meilin's injury would allow.

"We must hurry!" she urged.

"What are those things!" Meilin demanded.

"Yuàn Guǐ—the tormented trapped souls of the children the spider demon took, who've yet to find solace and release!"

"Oh my God! And who are you!"

"I'm the spider demon."

Meilin instantly yanked her hand free from the ghost girl's. She brought her bo staff up, ready to strike.

But she couldn't. This girl wasn't the spider demon—she couldn't be! She was young and despite her ghostly appearance, quite beautiful.

Yet, somehow Meilin knew that she was.

"You can strike me down if you wish," the ghost girl said. "I won't contest it. But please, hear my story first. Help me put an end to all that's happened before it goes on any longer. I beg you!"

Meilin didn't know what to do. She wanted to vanquish the spider demon with a vengeance and put an end to it forever.

But *that* was the Darkness of the Shadow Realm talking in her brain. Meilin knew she had to fight against the negative energy that permeated everything in this god-forsaken land; otherwise she would succumb to its dark power.

"The Shadow Realm is not evil," Xiao Hong once told her. *"Yet evil readily abounds there."*

To survive in the Shadow Realm, Meilin knew she needed to maintain control over her inner Tao. She had to maintain her balance—otherwise she would be lost in the Shadow Realm—forever.

Meilin's demon monkey-senses tingled again. The light from the orb the ghost girl created had dissipated. The relentless Yuàn Guǐ were coming again, and this time, Meilin could feel, with even more determination and anger.

With a tremendous effort, Meilin spun in place to face them. She raised her bo staff, ready to fight—and then she collapsed to the ground. All of her strength was gone. The spider demon's poison had spread everywhere and her body was failing her fast. Even here in the Shadow Realm, where she thought she might be momentarily safe, she felt her world going dark.

Chapter 12

Meilin didn't know how many minutes, hours or days had passed before she opened her eyes again. She was completely disoriented and still feeling weak.

Laying on a bed of straw, she struggled to sit up, but found she couldn't. Meilin didn't have any strength at all. It took everything she could muster just to roll her head to the side and try to focus on her whereabouts.

She was still in the cave, she reasoned—but no longer in the Shadow Realm. Yet, she wasn't back in her natural realm, either. She was somewhere else.

"You're awake," a calm and soothing voice said.

An old man came into view above her. He had a kind face, a very long white beard, grey hair and he was dressed in a dark red-orange monk's robe. Meilin knew in her fuzzy mind that she'd seen him someplace before, but she just couldn't place it.

"Where am I?" Meilin whispered.

"You are—*here*," the old man said gently, gesturing with his hands.

"There was a girl... White face..."

"Ruomei," the old man smiled.

The ghost girl came into Meilin's view at the sound of her name and took her place beside the old man.

"You're lucky she found you."

Meilin closed her eyes. She remembered—the Yuàn Guǐ. She also remembered...

"The children! I have to save them!" she cried, with a renewed effort to rise. Again, her body failed her.

"Indeed. The children need saving," the old man said. "But, I'm afraid you're of no use to them—anymore."

Meilin let go a heavy sigh. If only her mother were here. Lijuan would know how to draw the spider venom out of her. But her mother was thousands of miles away—and thousands of years in the future.

Tears began to trickle from the corners of Meilin's eyes. She was the Monkey King's daughter, able to do almost anything—yet here she lay, helpless, unable to move.

"Why do you cry?" the old man asked.

"I don't know," Meilin replied, feeling slightly ashamed.

"Is it that you feel sorry for yourself," the old man prompted.

"No..." Meilin sniffled. Then she said with honesty, "Yes. A little... But mostly, I feel sorry because I failed. I failed the children."

"Failure is the foundation of success," the old man said.

"Tell that to *them*," Meilin replied, with heavy defeat in her voice.

Meilin then summoned her courage and asked, "Am I dying?"

The old man didn't answer.

Meilin closed her eyes at his silent proclamation.

"Does death frighten you?" the old man said.

Meilin looked up at him, then away.

"Yes," she admitted. Indeed, Dying *did* frighten her. "Yet somehow," Meilin then reflected, "it also doesn't." Meilin turned her head back to the old man, "I can't explain why, but..."

The old man smiled and nodded his head. *"All creatures in the universe return to the point from which they began. Returning to the source is tranquility. Being one with Heaven, we become one with the Tao. Being one with the Tao, we are no longer concerned with losing our life because the Tao is eternal.*"

The old man then added, "*Life and death are but one thread, viewed from different sides.*"

"My Uncle Z once told me that," Meilin said, forcing a smile. "But I guess I didn't understand what he meant—until now..."

"For a fat old pig, Zhu Bajie can be pretty wise at times."

"Then, you know who I am?"

"Yes," the old man said quietly. "Just as you know—who *I* am."

Meilin's eyes widened a bit.

"Mountain Deity."

The old man confirmed her words with a slow nod.

Meilin's jaw tightened and she grit her teeth as sudden anger welled inside her.

"How could you let this happen!" Meilin snapped. "For 900 years you've let those children die! The people prayed to you for help—yet you did nothing!"

Mountain Deity raised his hand, commanding Meilin's attention.

"Meilin," Mountain Deity said, his voice still calm, taking no offence at Meilin's outburst. "You misunderstand the extent of my being. I'm an earth deity. I'm of this mountain and all that flows from it. I'm not a demon or a man. Therefore, I do not walk among the living as you do. I cannot take the life of the living—nor the dead, no matter how just it may seem."

"But you *can* withhold your blessings! These people are starving. Where's the water your mountain can provide! Where's the compassion and aid you can give them when the people pray for your help!"

"Don't blame Mountain Deity for this!" Ruomei, interrupted. "This mountain's under a spell! My husband, the man you know as Gao, is the cause of all this!"

"Why!" Meilin demanded.

"Because he wants to save my life!"

"What!" Meilin spat. "But you're..."

"Dead. Yes, I know," Ruomei said. "But, my husband refuses to let me go."

Ruomei then knelt at Meilin's side. "900 years ago, my husband was not like the man you see today. He was a good man, with a good heart. He was studying magic and wanted to become a Taoist priest when we met. We fell in love. He abandoned his training and we married. We wanted to have children, raise a family. But one day, while picking flowers in the forest, I was bitten by a poisonous spider. There was nothing our village shaman could do. I was dying. Then, my husband heard about a mountain where, legend said, by drinking from the magical waters that flowed from the Mountain Deity's shrine, anyone could be cured. He rushed me here, but the journey was long and he was too late. I died taking my first sip from the blessed pool. And yet, because I took that one sip while dying, my soul wasn't completely released. My husband went insane with grief. He used the magic he'd learned to curse the shrine and all that came from it. His love for me turned to anger and hate for this mountain and its people. My love turned to anger and rage because I couldn't pass on. I was torn apart into two beings—my spirit—as you see me here—and the other. Because of the spider venom in my blood, my mortal body began to decay and mutate into the spider that's been preying on the village children ever since."

"But why?" Meilin demanded.

"Because, my husband believes that if he can feed me enough ch'i from innocent souls, he can bring me back to life. That's why he was so intent on deceiving you. Once he sensed you were fae— he had to have you. Your ch'i is worth the ch'i of a thousand human beings. Enough to bring me back. Only he's wrong. All he'll succeed in doing is giving near immortality to the spider. And I'll go on killing forever. "

"Oh my God!" Meilin gasped.

"You could've ended this by killing me, Meilin! Had you seen through Gao's guise—had you killed the demon spider when you had the chance, my soul—and the souls of the Yuàn Guǐ—would have been released."

Meilin sighed heavily and closed her eyes.

"I'm sorry," she said. "But, even if I'd had the opportunity, I know deep inside, I wouldn't have killed you. I'd have found another way. Killing is against my Tao."

"Even if it means saving the lives of the six who've yet to die?"

Meilin slowly draped her arm across her face to hide her tears. So, there was still time to save the six children from the demon spider after all. New Year's Eve had yet to come.

But Meilin had already lost her battle. She was dying—all because of her arrogant pride in her ability, and her foolish assumption that she was above the natural laws of the Tao. Her Uncle Z was right. What Meilin initially wanted to achieve—to restore Jessie's grandmother—was wrong, no matter how noble her reasoning might be. And now, six more children would suffer for her mistakes. Six children she could have saved...

"To become whole, you must first be broken," Mountain Deity said. *"To become straight, you*

must first be twisted. To become full, you must first let yourself become empty."

Mountain Deity then made a quick circular gesture with his hands and placed them on Meilin's body, one on her head, and the other on her wound. Blinding white light erupted from his palms and fingertips and penetrated Meilin's body, deep into the very essence of her being. Meilin felt her life miraculously returning as her entire body and soul was filled with life-giving Yang.

"Meilin, you sought to learn the Way of the Healing Hand for all the wrong reasons," Mountain Deity pronounced. "You sought to alter that which cannot be changed. You lacked humility and true virtue. You haven't begun to comprehend the nature of the Tao. And yet," he then said, in a gentler tone, "I see that your heart and mind are pure and open. Your ch'i is strong. You're worthy of the long journey you're taking. Therefore, I'm going to give you the healing knowledge you sought. And with it, I give you something more. Use my gifts wisely..."

Chapter 13

When Meilin materialized back in the cave, she found both Gao and the spider demon still enraged with her sudden disappearance.

That meant that the time Meilin spent in the Shadow Realm, and the time she spent in the sanctuary of Mountain Deity's presence, was only but a few moments of real time. New Year's Eve had yet to transpire—there was still time to save the children!

"Looking for me?" Meilin called, as she went full monkey, morphing into her demon monkey-state. Her longest jade hair stick flew into her hands and changed to bo staff size.

Meilin had materialized several yards behind Gao and the demon and was ready for action. Mountain Deity had mercifully restored her life and given her a second chance. She was determined not to waste the gift he had granted.

"You!" Gao cried, spinning around. "I don't know how you escaped, but your monkey tricks won't save you again!"

"Gao! Listen to me!" Meilin demanded. "That demon is not your wife! Ruomei's dead! She died 900 years ago!"

"Liar!" Gao screamed defiantly. "Ruomei's alive—as you can plainly see!"

"No!" Ruomei said, materializing from the Shadow Realm at Meilin's side. "I'm not!"

The ghost girl floated toward her husband and the seething spider demon.

"Husband," Ruomei begged. "Look at me! Can't you see what you've done? Can't you see what I've become? If you ever loved me—you must let me go. Put an end to this horror, I beg you!"

"Argh!" Gao spat. "You're not my wife! You're a trick—a monkey girl trick! Ruomei is alive! I WILL have her alive—*forever!*"

And with that, Gao charged Meilin, passing right through Ruomei's spirit form, with murder in his eyes.

The spider demon, too, hissed and reared up on her four hind legs. She charged forward, determined to grab and envelop Meilin again in her sticky web of death.

Meilin was ready for them both.

Meilin parried the downward cutting stroke of Gao's sword with a fast upward motion of her jade bo staff, easily slapping the blade aside. She then reversed her feet and brought the momentum of her bo back and across her body, hitting the spider demon on the left side of her thorax as the demon tried to rush to Melin's exposed side.

The spider demon spun away from the force of Meilin's blow. Meilin then whipped her staff back behind her right shoulder, brought her hands together, and swung it like a baseball bat at both Gao and the spider demon simultaneously to drive them back. She wanted a little more space between her and her adversaries.

Meilin continued her circular momentum as she spun herself low to the ground in an attempt to sweep Gao's feet out from under him.

But Gao was nimble and quickly jumped up and away.

Meilin anticipated the move. As Gao jumped, Meilin planted the tip of her staff into the ground and launched her own body forward, using her staff as support. She side-kicked Gao square in his sternum with her extended right leg. The force of Meilin's kick sent him flying hard against the cavern wall.

At the same time as Meilin executed her kick, the spider demon hooked the tip of Meilin's bo staff with one of her longer legs and pulled it out from under her.

Meilin fell to the ground, but rolled easily to her feet.

Immediately, Meilin's two smaller jade hair sticks flew from her ponytail knot, grew, and fixed themselves to the end of her bo. The bo immediately shrank to jo staff size, creating Meilin's sanjiegun—the Chinese three-section fighting staff.

Gao and the spider demon regrouped and charged Meilin again.

This time, Meilin didn't wait. She raced forward and met them head-on.

Meilin attacked the spider demon first. Utilizing the outer sections of her sanjiegun like two escrima fighting sticks, she pummeled and blocked the demon's many arms with a flurry of lightning-fast blows that sent the spider demon reeling backward.

Meilin then spun up into the air and let her hands slide to one end of her sanjiegun and brought it down like a whip, cracking it atop the spider demon's hideous head—dropping her to the ground.

Gao attempted to rush Meilin from the rear and slash her across her back with his sword, but Meilin spun in place, reset her grip, and used the center section of her sanjiegun to block his blade. She then smashed Gao twice across his face with her sanjiegun's outer ends.

As Gao hurriedly back-stepped in an effort to avoid being hit again, Meilin whipped her sanjiegun around her waist like a long baton to build up speed—jumped up in the air and brought her weapon down hard, cracking Gao across his ribcage.

In the same motion, Meilin back-kicked the spider demon in her face as she tried to rush in.

As Meilin delivered her kick, she dropped into a tight summersault and rolled into Gao while collapsing all three sections of her staff into a tight bundle. Meilin then shot to her feet and rammed the three ends of her folded staff hard under Gao's jaw, sending him flying, near senseless, to the ground.

Again the spider rushed Meilin. Without looking, Meilin let her sanjiegun fly up over her head, extending the three sections to their full length. The business end of the staff then arced down over Meilin and delivered a crushing blow across the spider demon's neck and back.

Meilin then spun and again, using a whirling figure-eight pattern, pummeled the spider demon relentlessly, driving her back toward the center of the cave.

The spider demon, having had enough, leapt up to the safety of the cavern roof and scurried for cover among the dark crevices.

Meilin turned her attention back to Gao, who slowly struggled to his feet.

The ghost-form of his wife, Ruomei, was already at his side. Though she could not physically touch him in her ethereal state, she nonetheless tried.

"Husband!" Ruomei pleaded, "Stop this madness! I beg you!"

"Listen to her, Gao!" Meilin cried. "It's over! You've lost. Let her go in peace!"

"Never!" Gao raged, pushing himself to his feet, using his sword as a crutch. "Do you think it was easy? Living in isolation for 900 years—eating rats and vermin—masquerading as a demon hunter every thirty—protecting Ruomei—making certain she could harvest enough children to stay alive until I gathered enough ch'i and magic to bring her back?"

Gao threw down his sword in disgust.

"I didn't do this for myself!" Gao cried. "I did it for her!"

"No," Ruomei's ghost countered. "You did this for yourself! And look at what we've become! Both of us—so consumed with anger that our love's turned to hate!"

"Enough!" Gao roared.

"Enough of your monkey magic!" he directed at Meilin. He then hissed at the apparition that floated before him, "You're not real! You're not my wife!"

Gao slowly raised both his arms up from his sides. His hands started to glow. The cave floor around him began to tremble. Chunks of rocks began to loosen and rise.

"You like magic, monkey girl!" Gao ranted. "I'll show you what 900 years of my magic can do!"

Gao then wailed. "Ruomei! Take the children— now!"

Immediately the spider demon reappeared from the safety of the crevices at the far end of the cave. It leapt onto the side of the cavern walls and scurried across for the six silk-encased children.

"Oh, snap!' Meilin cussed. Her mind raced, calculating who to take on first—Gao or the demon.

"You stop Gao!" the ghost of Ruomei cried, making the decision for her. "I'll stop the demon!"

"But—" Meilin objected.

"Trust me!" Ruomei pleaded as she vanished.

With a tremendous cry, Gao willed the floating rocks and stone to fly across the cave at Meilin. Meilin spun in place and reformed her jade bo staff. With whirlwind speed, she expertly deflected all the rocks and stones that came screaming at her.

At the same time, just as the spider demon reached her prizes, Ruomei's ghostly form flew into the spider demon's body. The spider demon twisted and contorted as Ruomei struggled to repossess her corrupted form. Through shear will, Ruomei kept the spider demon from taking and devouring her prey. But it was a battle Ruomei knew she could not win. The spider demon was filled with dark Yin and she was losing control.

"Meilin!" Ruomei cried.

But Meilin had her own hands full. Gao had gathered a lot of magic in his many years of insane existence—and he was determined to use it all!

Gao formed a tight ball of swirling dark crimson and purple energy and cast it out at Meilin.

"Die!" he shrieked.

"Gao! No!" Meilin commanded, as the deadly energy ball came straight for her.

Meilin thrust her jade bo staff out before her to stop the orb. Her bo staff, created by her grandmother, Guan Yin, had been infused with pure celestial magic. The tip of her bo erupted with a white-blue light that shot forth and intercepted Gao's ball of deadly negative energy midway between them.

"Gao!" Meilin urged. "Let it go!"

But Gao wouldn't. He summoned every ounce of dark magic he could muster and directed it into his menacing orb.

But Meilin wouldn't be deterred. Her ch'i was far stronger than Gao's and she was filled with positive life-giving Yang.

The swirling and pulsating sphere grew in size until it finally exploded! The shockwave from the massive blast blew everyone, Gao, Meilin, and the spider demon, off their feet.

Gao took the brunt of the explosion. The negative energy he had cast at Meilin returned to his body in full force.

Gao collapsed to the ground—his body and his magic—spent.

Meilin gaped at her jade bo staff, both shocked and amazed at its power. This was not something she expected. What had her grandmother *really* given her?

"Ruomei!" Meilin then suddenly thought, as she reverted to her human-form. Her jade bo instantly morphed to hair stick size and returned to her ponytail knot.

Ruomei lay crumpled on the ground, near the six silk-encased children. The spider demon took a serious blow from the explosion, but the Yang that emanated throughout the cave from the blast was enough to change its corrupted body back to human form.

At least, half way.

The spider demon's eight long limbs, broken and twisted, still projected from Ruomei's back.

Meilin ran to her side and gathered her up in her arms.

"Kill me! I beg you!" Ruomei pleaded, as Meilin held her close.

"I can't!" Meilin replied. "You know I can't. It's against my Tao."

"You must—or I'll go on killing forever!"

"No!" Meilin cried, tears running down her cheeks. "There still has to be another way!"

From the far corner of the cave, Gao slowly opened his eyes. Seeing Meilin cradling Ruomei in her arms, her back turned, he saw his chance.

Gao ushered of all his strength to push himself up to a kneeling position. His body, without the magic to sustained it, was rapidly aging. But he still had some strength inside. Gao slowly drew his dagger from his belt—and threw it at Meilin.

Meilin didn't see it coming, but Ruomei did. Using her broken spider limbs, she pulled Meilin into her chest as she turned.

Gao's dagger entered deep into Ruomei's back, piercing her heart.

Ruomei slumped to the ground, releasing Meilin.

"NO!" Meilin cried with disbelief. "Ruomei!"

But it was too late.

Meilin gazed down into Ruomei's watery eyes. There was absolute contentment on her face.

"Thank you, Meilin," Ruomei whispered with her final breath. "Thank you..."

Ruomei's beautiful dark eyes went blank.

She was dead.

"Nooo! Gao screamed in utter despair, realizing that he had killed his wife. "Nooo!"

Gao crumpled in place. It was all he could do to claw at the earth as he dragged his withering body across the cave in a desperate effort to reach her side.

The haunting voices of hundreds of children suddenly filled Meilin's ears, crying out from the darkness of the Shadow Realm.

Ruomei's 900 years of torture and anguish were over. Her spirit—and the spirits of the Yuàn Guǐ—were finally free.

As the ghostly din faded, Ruomei's spirit reappeared—this time, a far different apparition than her previous pale ghost form.

Ruomei radiated with ethereal lightness and beauty as she stood over Gao's decaying body.

She knelt at his side as he used the last ounce of his strength to roll onto his back.

"Ruomei!" Gao whispered hoarsely. "I loved you..."

"As I loved you, my husband—with all my heart, Ruomei said. Glittering tears of light trickled down her face as she spoke. "But I died. We all die. It's the nature of things."

"Will I ever—see your face again?" Gao choked.

"Perhaps—in another life—if Buddha is merciful," Ruomei replied softly. "But, we both have *so much* to atone for..."

"Remember me, if you can," Gao begged.

"I will... if I can, my love," Ruomei promised.

Ruomei then leaned gently forward to kiss Gao. As their lips touched, she faded away.

Gao's body then began to tremble and shake as death finally took him. Within seconds, his body rapidly aged the last of his 900 years—and turned to dust.

Chapter 14

Chun, her daughter, Pei, and the rest of the mothers of the village who had lost their children, held silent vigil at the shrine of Mountain Deity, praying for Meilin's safe return.

Though they had done as Meilin instructed and left the village the evening before, they disregarded her instructions to stay away until someone—hopefully Meilin, sent word that it was safe to return.

Instead, the women had returned early in the morning and made their way up the mountain to the shrine in order to pray for her.

It was now nearing noon on New Year's Day. The grim reality of the truth was woefully apparent—Meilin was not coming back. The young girl who had come into their lives, convinced that she could do what no other could do for 900 years, had failed.

The glimmer of hope that Meilin offered the mothers of the lost was just that—a glimmer. Now, that glimmer was gone.

The women, their eyes moist, but tearless, bowed to the effigy of Mountain Deity. They slowly rose, resigned to their continuing fate. Only little Pei cried openly.

As they turned to start the long walk down the mountain back to the village, and another 30-years of living in misery and dread, little Pei remained momentarily behind.

As a farewell gesture, Pei removed the jade Monkey King necklace that Meilin had given her from around her neck and gently placed it into the statue's open cupped palm.

"You like that?" Pei remembered Meilin asking softly.

Pei remembered shaking her head, yes.

She remembered Meilin smiling, reaching around to the back of her neck and undoing its tiny silver clasp.

Pei remembered Meilin saying, *"Then it's yours,"* as Meilin fastened it around her neck. *"I want you to have it. Something to remember me by."*

Pei put her hands together and bowed one last time to Mountain Deity.

Finally, she too, turned away, resigned to the knowledge that her new sister, that strange brave girl who had saved her life—was gone.

Pei only took one step, when she heard a curious sound. She turned around and stared.

Water—first a trickle, then a steady stream, had begun to flow from the crack in the rocks.

"Momma!" Pei called.

The timber of Pei's voice made Chun stop and turn around.

Chun's eyes widened, as she too, saw the basin at Mountain Deity's feet begin to fill with water.

All the women stopped and turned to see.

Where their eyes deceiving them?

Could it be?

Then the women heard another sound—this one from higher up the trail.

The women turned, their hearts in their throats, hoping beyond all hope as six children, dazed, famished, but otherwise alive, made their way slowly down the mountain trail from the cave above.

Chapter 15

Meilin stood next to Jessie, holding her hand tightly, in the back of the hospital room. Standing next to Meilin was her uncle, Zhu Bajie, and her mother, Lijuan.

Jessie's mother, Grace, and her father, Eric, were at her grandmother's bedside when the attending physician shook his head and pronounced that Jessie's grandmother was gone.

Jessie's mom immediately broke down into uncontrollable tears. Eric did his best to comfort her.

Jessie also started to cry and leaned into Meilin for support.

Lijuan stepped forward and helped Eric lead Grace gently from the room. Zhu Bajie, in turn, moved to guide both Jessie and Meilin from the room as well.

Lijuan paused at the doorframe as Eric and Grace went on ahead. She turned and held out her hand as Meilin approached. Her expression was cold.

Meilin knew that look.

Without hesitation Meilin reached up to her ponytail knot and withdrew her three jade hair sticks. Without protest, she silently placed them into her mother's open palm.

Lijuan closed her fingers tightly around the hair sticks while staring at her daughter. Meilin had openly disobeyed Lijuan and had broken the immeasurable trust that was given her. There were consequences to every action—this was one of them. Meilin was sure there would be plenty more before she regained her mother's trust again and the right to possess the keys to her heritage.

Lijuan then turned and walked swiftly to rejoin the grieving Grace and Eric, leaving Meilin, Jessie, and Zhu Bajie behind.

Meilin looked up at her Uncle.

"Can Jessie and I have a minute, please?" Meilin asked softly.

Zhu Bajie considered her request for a long moment, then nodded his head and smiled.

"I'll be down the hall," he said, closing the door, leaving the two girls alone in the room.

Jessie turned and looked back at the body of her grandmother.

"If only I could have told her one last time that I loved her," Jessie sobbed. "I didn't hate her, Meilin. I really didn't!"

"I know you didn't," Meilin said, hugging her friend. "I know..."

Meilin then took Jessie by her hand and led her to her grandmother's bed.

"I'm going to share a gift with you, Jess," Meilin said. "So don't be afraid."

Meilin took one of Jessie's hands and joined it with her grandmother's, holding both between her palms.

"This will only last a few moments," she said. "So use your time wisely.

A blinding white light then emanated from Meilin's hands.

Meilin then left the room and closed the door, leaving Jessie inside.

After a few minutes, the door reopened, and Jessie emerged. There were tears on her face, but Meilin knew they weren't solely tears of sorrow. They were also tears of joy.

The two girls hugged for a long moment. Meilin then took Jessie by her arm and they started to walk slowly down the hall, where an approving Zhu Bajie stood waiting.

"I tried to tell her I was sorry," Jessie said, "But she stopped me. She said that she was the one who was sorry—sorry for all the anger that she had deep inside herself that kept her from loving us. She wasn't mad at us. She was mad at herself because she didn't know how to let it go. She was mad for something that happened when my mother married my father sixteen years ago—a silly argument that grew and festered inside her, making her unable to express her love. Oh, Meilin, Grandma loved us—she always did. But she didn't know how to tell us. Her anger at herself got in the way!"

"Anger is a bitter enemy," Meilin said. "As long as it lives inside you, you can never be who you really are. You can never be at peace with yourself—or the world."

"Thank you, Meilin," Jessie sniffled, leaning her head onto Meilin's shoulder as they walked. "I only wish my mom and dad were in the room with me to hear what Grandma's spirit had to say."

Meilin smiled. "Don't worry," she replied. "Your grandma's spirit will come to them tonight in a dream. When they wake in the morning, they'll remember—and find peace."

"You can do that?" Jessie said with surprise. "My God, what happened to you while you were gone?"

Meilin shrugged. "It's a long story. Let's just say, I learned something the hard way: To become whole, you must first be broken. To become straight, you must first be twisted. To become full, you must first let yourself become empty."

"And what's all that supposed to mean?" Jessie asked.

"It means," Meilin replied, "that I really don't know anything about who I am, who I can become—the Tao—anything. I have to start over at the beginning and I've got a whole lot of learning to do..."

"And I'm looking forward to every second of it," Meilin finished silently.

Meilin then smiled with anticipation, in her own monkey way.

Glossary

Butsudan *(but-sue-dan)* literally *Buddha altar*, a wooden cabinet with doors that enclose and protect a religious image of the Buddha.

Ch'i *(chee)* internal life force. Also written as **Chi** or **Qi**

Chinese bao *(bao, as in <u>bow</u> down)* a steamed bun or dumpling.

Chun *(chuen)* a female name meaning spring, love, life (depends on inflection).

Duangua *(dwan-gwa)* mandarin-styled Tai Chi or Kung fu jacket worn by men or women.

Escrima *(es-krim-ah)* stick fighting. Escrima sticks are between 26" and 28" long with a diameter of 1" to 1 ¼."

Fae *(fay)* fairy folk.

Guan Yin *(gwan yin)* Taoist Goddess of Mercy.

Hong Hai-Er *(honh hi ar)* Red Boy. Son of Demon Bull King and Princess Iron Fan.

Hong Bao *(honh bao)* Red Packet. An envelope containing money, given as a gift for good luck.

Huli-jing *(huli jing)* A Chinese fairy fox-spirit trickster, usually female, that can be good or bad.

Lijuan *(lee-jewan)* a female name meaning beautiful and graceful.

Logograms *(logo-grams)* visual symbols representing words, rather than sounds or phonemes that make up a word.

Meilin *(may-lin)* a female name meaning beautiful jade or plum jade.

Mount Huaguo *(hwa-gwo-ah)* The Mountain of Flowers and Fruit.

Pei *(pay)* a female name meaning teach, admire or rain (depends on inflection).

Penglai *(pung-lai)* a fabled Fairy Isle on the China Sea.

Ruomei *(zhruh-may)* a female name meaning, "like a plum."

Sanjiegun *(san-jeh-gwun)* the Chinese three-section fighting staff.

Shuilian-dong *(shway-lee-ann dohn)* The fabled Water Curtain Cave. Home of the monkey kingdom.

Sifu *(she-fu)* respectful term used for master or teacher. Also written as **Shifu**.

Sun Wukong *(swun wukong)* The Monkey King [*Sun* monkey + *Wu* awareness + *Kong* vacuity, *Wukong* awakened to emptiness.]

Tao *(dao)* (in Chinese philosophy) the absolute principle underlying the universe, combining within itself the principles of yin and yang and signifying the way, or code of behavior, that is in harmony with the natural order. The interpretation of Tao in the Tao-Te-Ching developed into the philosophical religion of Taoism. [The Way or Path.] It stresses humility, compassion and moderation.

Xiao-Hong *(shao hong)* a female name meaning morning rainbow.

Yang (in Chinese philosophy) the active male principle of the universe, characterized as creative and associated with heaven, heat, and light.

Yin (in Chinese philosophy) the passive female principle of the universe, characterized as sustaining and associated with earth, dark, and cold.

Yin Yang yin and yang are complementary opposites within a greater whole. In Asian philosophy, *everything* has both yin and yang aspects, which constantly interact, change and are never static.

Yuàn Guǐ (yuan gway) the spirits of those who died wrongful deaths. They cannot go to the Chinese Underworld for reincarnation. They roam the world, waiting for a mortal to free them.

Wu Shi (wu shee) Lion Dance.

Wushu (wu shoo) Chinese martial arts.

Zhu Bajie *(jou ba-jeh)* aka Pigsy the Pig. An immortal turned into a pig-demon for breaking the prohibitions of Buddhism. *[Zhu* pig + *Ba* eight + *Jie* prohibitions.]

To read more books in the series and follow

THE MANY ADVENTURES OF MEILIN

THE MONKEY KING'S DAUGHTER

visit your favorite bookstore
or log on to:

themonkeykingsdaughter.com

CPSIA information can be obtained at www.ICGtesting.com
Printed in the USA
LVOW111733031111

253407LV00001B/121/P